The Mystery

Of MI-5's

Missing

Treasure

To Shari,
I hope you enjoy my book
as much as I
enjoyed writing it.
Michele

J.M.M. ADAMS

Apple Cove Press

Cover Artist: Roslyn McFarland
Editor: Richard Perfrement

www.jmmadams.com

Titles by J.M.M. ADAMS

Kanani's Golden Caves

Sophia and the Stradivarius (Appearing in First String an Indie Film)

Sophia and the Dragon

The Russian Spy

The Mystery of Sandy Island

The Mystery of St. Moritz

Be sure to check out Michele's blogs and books at
www.jmmadams.com
Http://amzn.to2bhoEeZ

CONTENTS

This book is Dedicated to all

Canines in the military,

Police dept., and other departments;

keeping us

Safe from evil.

May God always look over them with

protection

and love.

1

WE WERE IN the attic of the old house in Cornwall, Tintagel, England. Casey quickly looked for a window to air out the musty smell and get some fresh air for us.

We had just arrived by car from Hampshire, England about a 4-hour ride. Casey and I had visited an Aunt she didn't know she had, which would have been Casey's father's sister. He didn't know about her either! Casey was left without parents when both of hers had gone down in a private plane over Russia 20 years ago. Casey was 27 now, she had been raised by her mother's parents. They lived in Friday Harbor, WA, a scenic small island in the strait of Juan de Fuca, where Casey and I had lived for a long time before we got our first big assignment to find Sophia and Kanani, what an adventure that was. Back to the attic and why we are here......Opps, Casey was calling me.

I'm coming Casey, I got busy with this box. I lifted my head out of the box and joined her.

"I found this old desk, Jackie Lee." Casey wiped the thick layer of dust off the top and tried the drawers.

"Darn, they're all locked." She looked around for something to pry it open. "I'm going down to the kitchen to find a tool or screwdriver Jackie Lee; you can stay here or join me buddy." Casey rubbed my ears.

I trotted after her, we got down into the kitchen. There was a gas stove, wooden cabinets on both sides of the sink. There was a French country table with 6 chairs around it. The table was empty. There was an icebox, Casey opened it. That was empty as well. Then she looked in the drawers under the cabinets. There was some silverware sitting in trays, a cork screw, wine opener and ice trays.

"Jackie Lee let's go check out that bedroom." I followed her out of the kitchen and we took a left turn into the bedroom, it had a big bathroom attached.

It was a cute little cottage in Tintagel, about an hour south of Devon, it sat overlooking a bluff. Cornwall was beautiful! It was a stone cottage with a thatched roof, it was surrounded by a rock fence, and there were red, yellow, violet, well, just about every flower color in the garden. Casey said they were wild flowers. The front door was a red wooden door, there were windows on both sides of the front, then around the side by the kitchen, there was a huge window. Probably so you could look at the view. Inside, the floors were cobblestone, it was sparsely furnished, with an antique writing desk under the window overlooking the bluff. A small leather couch facing the desk and view, then one giant wooden rocking chair. From the living room, you could turn right and walk into a small bedroom. Since we were coming from the kitchen we turned left. It was furnished with a brass bed and a blue down comforter. There was a night stand with a lamp, then an antique clothes closet.

Casey walked over and opened it. There wasn't anything in there except a wooden box in the far-left corner. She reached down and picked it up. Looking inside she got a grin on her face; then looked at me.

"The keys to the desk Jackie Lee." She reached for them and took them out, showing them to me. "These should work."

I followed her back out into the living room and up the stairs to the attic. Casey put one of the keys into the locked drawer, it opened. I was holding my breath; I was so excited to be here. That meeting with Casey's aunt was weird to be sure. She told us a story that was almost unbelievable.

The drawer opened and Casey reached inside. She pulled out an envelope, it was a big yellow one. She dumped the contents onto the desk top. There were sealed letters, pictures and documents. Casey opened the other drawers and they were full of the same, then in the last drawer there was a map with markings on it. Casey pulled that out too. Casey looked around and found a basket, she dumped the contents out and shoved all of the things on the desk into it.

"Let's take this downstairs, Jackie Lee, where we can be comfortable. I'll make some ice and we can have some cold water. I'll need to go to the market and get some food for us. We will be using this as our base camp until we go through all of this and I can give Aunt Claire a report. Then it would be fun to go through Tintagel Castle. Do you know that is where our Sophia, Kanani, Gunther and all the others are living in another time? I wonder if this house is the one Sophia had built? Wouldn't that be something?" Casey grabbed the basket and started down the stairs, I followed her.

That would be really something if we found something here from Sophia! Who knows?

Casey placed the basket on the kitchen table, then took out the ice tray, filled it with water and placed in the freezer.

"We will have to get a modern frig. If we end up living here for any period of time. Aunt Claire said this house belonged to me, I must call Peter and let him know what we have found out so far. He could maybe come here while we go through everything, hmm, sounds like a plan, I'll talk to him." Casey looked pensive, then pulled out some paper and a pencil from her purse.

"Let me make a list of things we need Jackie Lee, you can stay home or come with me, but you'd have to sit in the car." She looked at me.

WOOF! I wagged my tail. I'm going, just leave the windows down, it's cool out. I want to see the area!

"OK! I get!" Casey laughed. She finished the list then placed it in her bag. She started towards the front door, then grabbed my leash off a chair. "Just in case." She looked at me with a smile as my tail was thumping on the floor like an old English tattoo.

We had rented a little Mini Cooper S, it may have been a Mini but there was plenty of room for me as I jumped into the front seat. Casey put the key in the ignition and we pulled out of the driveway. I noticed there were other little cottages also lining the cliff. We took our time passing by them, it was such a beautiful place, after the houses came a little village. Casey pulled up in front of the market. She put the windows down and told me to stay.

Of course, I would stay! Only if she needed me would I jump out and go help.

I watched people walk by, they stared at me like they had never seen a German Shepherd before, I smiled with my teeth showing and people started pointing and laughing. Casey came out right about then.

A lady approached her. I heard her ask Casey what kind of dog I was. She said she wanted a dog for her kids. Casey invited her over to meet me.

"May I pet him?" she asked Casey.

"Yes, I'm here, he won't bite." Casey replied.

She gently pet me, "My kids would love you! Where do I get a dog like you?"

Casey put the groceries in the car. Then took out a business card, she wrote something on it and handed it to the lady.

"There's the website where Jackie Lee came from. I know the breeder; they are very nice people. Tell her I sent you." Casey said.

The lady looked at the card, "I will. Wow, you got him from Germany? Where in England would they ship a dog?" she asked.

"Probably London." Casey replied.

"You know I didn't introduce myself." The lady said. "I'm Sally McMasson, my husband is the chairman of the Tintagel Parish Council. If you need anything we can help you. Where are you staying?" Sally asked Casey.

"The Lane cottage, my name is Casey Lane and this is Jackie Lee. This was my grandparents place when they were alive. Do you know anything about my grandfather or the cottage?" Casey asked.

"Only that he was a very private man, said he worked in a bank in London until he retired. Your grandmother lived there until her passing 20 years ago. She was a lovely lady. She was kind to everyone." Sally said.

"Well thank you, I'll be in touch." Casey said shaking her hand. Casey was just getting into the car, when Sally handed her a slip of paper.

"My phone number, call sometime, we can have lunch and talk." Sally smiled.

"Thank you." Casey closed the door and started the car. She waved goodbye to Sally as we drove off heading back to the cottage.

"That was interesting Jackie Lee. I never knew these grandparents and neither did the grandparents I grew up with. I'm so confused how this could have happened. Then how did the cottage stay so neat and tidy? I must ask Aunt Claire how she found the cottage and found this stuff out." Casey drove on.

I didn't say anything. What could I add? It was weird.

We got back to the cottage and Casey let me help her carry in the groceries. We filled the fridge with fresh food and then filled up some of the cabinets with dry goods. Casey and I had plenty to eat. Casey had some trout for us to eat for dinner tonight. YUM.

Casey pulled out some ice cubes and plopped them into a bowl of water for me, then made herself a cold ice tea to drink. She took that and sat it on the table, then started going through the pile of papers in the basket. The table was long, so there was plenty of room on it for a dinner plate too.

"Look Jackie Lee!" Casey showed me a photo of her grandpa on a 1930 gangster car, he was standing on the side with a Carcano slung over his right shoulder. This was an Italian gun with a bolt action which was used during that time period. I know because Casey explained it to me.

She pulled out another photo. There was her grandpa with Aunt Claire as a child and another child too, a boy.

Then another photo with a woman who was probably Aunt Claire's mother.

HOLY COW what is going on?

I bet Casey wanted to know too.

Casey picked up her cell phone. "Hello, Aunt Claire we made it to the house. I've found loads of photos. Some are a bit confusing; did Grandpa have two wives?" Casey asked.

She had the phone on speaker.

"No dear, not at the same time. My mother disappeared during the war, down in Brazil. We never found her. When we were grown, and had our own families, father remarried. He kept us a secret from his new wife and kids. That would have been your grandma and your dad. He never told us about any of you. You see, Dad was working for MI-5 and we knew it, but I don't think any of you did." Claire paused.

"My dad would have been devastated to hear this, I wonder now if my dad wasn't murdered. The way he died in the plane crash with my mother never made any sense." Casey waited for Aunt Claire to speak.

"I would like to hear more about him too, Dear. I couldn't bear it anymore and went to find my father, that's when I found him living in Tintagel; I contacted him and he met with me. He told me all about his wife and your father, his son. I never got to meet your father and my brother has long since died, so I'm the only one left. We never got to meet our grandparents because of Dad being a spy." Claire waited for this to soak into Casey's mind a bit.

"My dad never got to meet his grandparents either or his father's sisters or brothers. My dad was told by his father that his father was an orphan. So many lies........." Casey was thinking.

"I know Dear, the pain I have felt, the pain your dad endured, then Meggie, your maternal grandmother, never knew about either of them. I'm sure it's because your dad was killed around the time his mother died and our father was long gone. Then Meggie, your grandma and Bob, your grandpa that raised you didn't know anything. We will talk more after you've had a chance to look through everything Dear. I would love to see the photos of my brother, mother and myself, that you found, perhaps you can bring them when you come back this way. I'm signing the title over to you Casey. You deserve this place more than I do. I'm old, and taken care of, you have your whole life ahead of you." Claire finished.

With tears in her eyes, Casey said goodbye and hung up.

She looked at me. "What a mess, let's find out why he went to Columbia. What was he doing there with his family? What happened to his first wife? So many questions. Oh, I need to call Peter, he must be worried sick." Casey picked her phone back up and called Peter.

"Peter?" Casey said.

She had the phone on speaker for me.

"Casey! Jackie Lee!" Peter was happy to hear from us.

WOOF, I barked wagging my tail.

"Hi Peter, how's Captain and T.J.? How are you feeling?" Casey asked.

"I'm feeling a lot bcttcr, the doctor told me I could go home soon. Casey? Where is home for me?" Peter asked.

Casey sighed, "Peter, I know what you mean. I just received ownership of this little cottage in Tintagel!"

"See what I mean, I have the condo in Switzerland, and on Sandy Island, you have a place in Coeur D'Alene and now in Cornwall." Peter laughed.

"Well,..... I guess I can go to my condo in

Switzerland and wait for you. Sandy Island is so far away right now." Peter paused.

"Peter, if you can fly, why don't you and the dogs come down here to Cornwall?" Casey offered.

"Only if you marry me there, Casey."

"Peter, you know I love you, but marriage right now is a bit overwhelming. Let me tell you what I've found out." Casey told Peter what had been happening since we arrived.

"That's some heavy stuff, as soon as I can get clearance to fly, we are on our way Casey."

"Peter?"

"Yes?"

"I'll marry you, come get us baby."

"Casey! I love you so much! I'll call you tomorrow, after my doctor's visit. You promise you will marry me?" Peter asked.

"Yes, I'm tired of being alone. I realize life is so complicated and short, the answer is yes." Casey blew him a kiss through the phone.

"Good night Casey. I love you." Then they hung up.

Casey looked at me. "Is that alright for you

Jackie Lee? You love Peter and T.J. and Captain too. We can all be a big family."

I jumped up and kissed her!

"Ok, let's go out." Casey said.

I was so happy and Casey was so preoccupied that we didn't notice the man watching us on the bluff behind us.

2

"JACKIE LEE, LET ME get your leash, let's go on a walk, I could use some fresh air."

Casey walked back inside grabbed my leash, her keys and locked the door. We walked out the little wood red gate and took a trip to the right of us, which was away from town but on the way to Tintagel Castle. On our right was a pasture with a farm in the distance. We passed some pretty big places, all of the homes were made of cobblestone and had rock fences. It was like out of a fairy tale. We passed a school house, then a little village of white stone houses.

"Look Jackie Lee, the sign says "Tintagel Castle 1 mile left at junction, ample parking. I think we should save this for another day, when it's a bit earlier. We'vc had a long day today." Casey turned around and we started back to our place.

A truck came around the corner fast; it

was coming right at us! I jumped on Casey and we landed on a patch of grass.

"Jackie Lee! That guy didn't even slow down! He tried to run us over!" Casey stood up and brushed herself off. "Thank you for saving me buddy. Are you hurt?" Casey ran her hands all up and down me.

I wagged my tail, I was OK, but she was going to be sore in the morning.

A car stopped and pulled over.

"Are you alright lady?" The man asked.

"I think so." Casey answered, as she limped over to his car.

"I saw that nut! He tried to run you down, I got his license plate number and called it in. At least there will be a report. Why don't you and your dog hop in, I'll take you home. Where are you staying?"

He got out and opened the back door for me, Casey sat in the front.

"Thank you for the lift and calling it in." Casey replied, "I'm Casey and he is Jackie Lee. We are just a mile down the road on the right."

His name was Scott, hmm just like the

Scott we knew from Liechtenstein. I was thinking. OH! What did he just say? I'd better listen.

"My brother in-law is the Police Chef and he doesn't put up with this stuff. We get so many tourists, it's been a big impact on this small town, but it has boosted the economy." Scott was saying.

"I bet, did you know Mr. James Lane or his wife Ethel?" Casey was fishing for information, I could tell.

"Yes, I remember them, it was a strange death for Mr. Lane and then his wife right after. They weren't that old. There was more to that than we ever found out. Why do you ask?" Scott inquired.

"I'm their granddaughter, I've just found out and been left their cottage. I just want to know more about them." Casey replied. "Ohh," Casey reached down and grabbed her ankle.

"Does it hurt?" Scott asked.

"Yes," Casey rubbed it. "I'll soak it tonight and hopefully it will be better."

"You have a nasty bruise forming on your

left arm too. Do you want me to run you down to the police station to make a statement and have you checked out by the nurse there? I really think it would be a smart idea Casey." Scott slowed down as he approached our cottage.

"Yes, perhaps we should, that's the cottage." Casey pointed.

"I know, I recognized it as soon as you mentioned their names. It will be nice to have someone young in it again. This is a lovely place to live and raise a family." Scott sped back up to drive us to the station. "Are you married Casey or have any kids?"

"No, but I did just get engaged and perhaps there will be a wedding in the near future." Casey smiled and looked at me.

I loved her so much, sigh, I missed T.J. and Captain. I couldn't wait until they got here!

We arrived at the station. Scott stopped the car and jumped out to help Casey limp into the station.

"Come on Jackie Lee, you can come too." Scott said as he opened the back door.

"Does he need a leash Casey?" Scott

asked.

"No not unless it's the law. He is very obedient. Aren't you Jackie Lee?" Casey bent over and rubbed my ears.

Woof! Yes, I am. Let's get this over with.

Casey gave her statement, Scott gave his account of it and Casey got checked out.

"You have a sprain, perhaps it's broken. That can't be determined until you get an x-ray. But here is some pain reliever and I've wrapped it. Here's some extra wrap for you to change it. If it still hurts in a few days, go to the Tintagel Medical Centre, let me write their number down for you." The nurse handed Casey a card with the Medical Centre's contact information and address.

"Thank you." Casey got up and limped out. Scott was waiting for us in the lobby.

"All set? Oh, you are hurt. Let me help you, I'll drive you two home." Scott took Casey's right arm and opened the station door; helping Casey out to his car.

It didn't take long of us to arrive at our cottage. Scott helped Casey out and helped her to the front door.

Casey pulled out her keys and put them in the lock. The door just swung open! Casey looked at Scott.

"I had it locked, someone is here or has been!" Casey backed away from the door.

"Let me go in and have look Casey." Scott offered.

"OK, if you're sure, we'll be right behind you." Casey followed Scott into the house. She was using me as a crutch of sorts.

Scott went into the bedroom and Casey waited outside the door.

"Someone has been in here; your suitcase is dumped out!" Scott came out and went into the kitchen.

"Casey!" Scott called her.

We walked into the kitchen. All of the photos and letters were dumped out on the floor.

Casey limped over and started picking things up, looking to see if anything was missing.

Casey! I don't see the map!

I sniffed around.

"Nothing is missing," Casey told Scott. "Could you please check the attic and bathroom for me? Would you like some tea?"

"I will check them out but not right now; I've got to get home and feed my dogs. Casey, let me push this heavy table against the kitchen door, then use something to block the front door tonight. I'll call a locksmith to come over in the morning and put an alarm in your home. His name is Mr. Jones and he is very fair and reasonable. Would that be OK?" Scott asked Casey.

"Yes, please do. We want to feel safe here." Casey added.

Scott decided his dogs could wait just a wee bit longer to be fed and went to check out the bedroom bathroom and the attic. "Nothing else is touched, do you feel comfortable to stay here tonight or do you want to go to a hotel?" Scott asked Casey.

"I have Jackie Lee, we can take care of ourselves, but thank you. Let me write my number down for you. Thank you so much for your kindness, Scott." Casey said.

"No problem, I'll check in on you tomorrow. I have to go to town anyway. Let me jot my number down for you and the police number. You should really report this." Scott scribbled the numbers down and handed them to Casey.

"I'll put a call in as soon as you leave." Casey said goodbye to Scott. He petted me and off he went.

Casey closed the door, the lock was busted. She picked up her cell phone and made a police report.

"Hello, my name is Casey Lane and I have a police matter to report. A hit and run. No, please just come by tomorrow morning. OK, thank you." Casey hung up.

"Jackie Lee, help me to push this heavy chair in front of the door." Casey limped over to the leather chair that sat under the desk in front of the window. With that being done; Casey went into the kitchen and whipped up some dinner for both us. We sat in the living room; Casey ate on the couch, placing her wine on the end table and her laptop on the coffee table in front of the couch. She turned on her laptop and started searching spy's during WWII, why would they go to Brazil?

"Jackie Lee, it makes no sense why someone is stalking us. It seems they don't want us messing with the background of my grandfather. It's been so many years, I just don't understand." Casey shook her head.

"Let's clean up, I'm going to soak in the tub and then we should get some sleep." Casey got up and took our dishes into the kitchen; she washed them in the sink and put them on a drying rack. She poured herself another glass of wine and limped into the bathroom connecting the bedroom.

While Casey was soaking in the tub, I heard a noise outside. I barked, raising my head to listen more intently.

Casey sat up. "Did you hear something boy?"

I woofed again and started growling as I walked slowly into the living room. There was someone looking in the window that overlooked the bluff!

3

CASEY WAS BEHIND me with a towel wrapped around her. She saw him too; he wasn't looking in the window but was digging in the garden!

Casey grabbed her cell phone and called the police, then got dressed. The police arrived without the sirens, as Casey had instructed. We watched it all from the window. The guy stopped digging, looked at the driveway and took off down the bluff! The police chased him, but he got away. They came back and talked to Casey. After they left, Casey and I went out to the garden that the man was digging in. She picked up the shovel and dug, thunk!

"I hit something Jackie Lee!"

I jumped into the hole and helped her dig.

Casey pulled out a small metal box. She wiped the dirt off the top and sides. She carried it into the house. In the kitchen by the sink, Casey washed it off.

"Jackie Lee, there's a lock on it. Go get the keys we found boy, they're on the desk by the window in the living room." Casey instructed. "Jackie Lee, I know you thought I forgot about that map, but I put it in my purse when we went out for our walk. It's safe." She smiled.

YES! I marched off to do my errand and came back with keys. Casey took them from me after giving me a treat for retrieving them.

She tried key after key with no luck, then just as she was about to get something to break it off, it opened with the last key!

Casey lifted the lid and pulled back. Inside was cash! It was all in Brazilian coins and paper money.

"I wonder how much this is? Why is it Brazilian currency and not pound sterling? Jackie Lee, why would Grandpa bury it and how did that person know of it?" Casey was confused.

"What's this?" She slipped her hands down through the money. There were photos and another map!

"I wonder what the maps stand for? I've

got to talk to Peter tomorrow. I need to find a WWII expert." Casey picked up the container and placed it under the bed.

Then she went back to her laptop and started googling historians on war crimes WWII.

"Jackie Lee, I found a man, Keith Schim, he leads a team of people that prosecute Nazi war criminals. I think maybe he can help us. I'll call there in the morning. He is in Germany, so let me see." Casey looked at time zones. "Germany is one hour ahead of us. I'll call first thing in the morning, then talk to Peter again. Let's go to bed." Casey closed her laptop, turned off the lights and we went to bed.

Than night I had a dream..........

Bombs were going off; I was in Germany with Casey. We were hunting a war criminal. Casey and I hid behind a tree; soldiers were passing by. They were English soldiers, they saw us.

"Hey Colonel!" Called a soldier, "come here."

A young soldier appeared, "What have we here?" he asked.

"Hi, we are just a bit lost." Casey said.

"Well! You can't stay out here, it's too dangerous. Come with us. Men! Get in line and let's get out of the woods!" The Colonel turned to go, "Oh, I'm Captain Lane and your names?" he asked.

Casey looked at me in wonder. "Casey and Jackie Lee," she answered.

"Hm, Lee is your last name. OK, Miss Lee follow us."

I looked at Casey, she shook her head as to warn me to be quiet.

We got to their headquarters. They put us up for the night.

"Jackie Lee, that's my grandfather when he was very young."

I know, this is way too weird.

The next morning, Colonel Lane came up to us.

"I've been reassigned to another position. The war is over, some of Germany just doesn't know it yet. I'm off to chase Nazi war criminals! You can't stay here, so you and your dog are being flown out of here with me back to

- 40 -

England. From there you can go wherever you're from. Follow me." Colonel Lane said good bye to the men and we followed him onto a helicopter.

Casey got to meet and talk to her future Grandfather, it was amazing.

I must have been running in my sleep because Casey shook me awake.

"Jackie Lee! WAKE UP! Wow, I wish I could have been in that dream." She rolled over and went back to sleep.

I couldn't get back to sleep, I just kept thinking about what Casey's Grandfather did with his life, where did he go? Was he chasing war criminals? Were the grandkids now after us? Why? So many questions.........

The next morning the police arrived and so did the alarm guy, Mr. Jones. He assured Casey that he would get a crew in that day and install it. The doors and windows had sensors; there was also a motion detector that would go on when we weren't home. The police added this report to the other one. Casey was still limping around.

She took me out into the back yard when

they installed the alarm and called Peter.

He answered on the first ring.

Casey put the phone on speaker for me.

"Hi sweetie, I was just going to call you. How are you doing?" Peter asked.

"OK now. Jackie Lee and I almost got run over on our walk last night, then our place was broken into, and after that another incident, a strange man digging in the garden at night who ran away when the police arrived. Jackie Lee and I checked out his digging and found something of interest buried too. I have an alarm going in right now." Casey barely finished and Peter was freaking out over the phone.

"Why didn't you call me last night?" he asked.

"What could you have done? You weren't here. I didn't want to worry you." Casey replied.

"Well, that's it, I'm getting a flight into England today then. I'll call you when I find out the landing time Casey. I'll rent a car so don't drive into London. I should arrive by tonight."

"Call me with the details Peter, Jackie Lee and I could drive in and get you." Casey offered.

Then she looked at her ankle and made a face.

"I forgot to tell you that I got hurt in the missed hit and run. I sprained my ankle and it's killing me, maybe you will need to get a ride here after all."

"Casey, you're scaring me girlfriend! We need to tie that knot so I can call you wife. I will call you right back." Peter signed off and Casey looked at me.

"It will be fun to have them here Jackie Lee. Hm, Peter will have to sleep on the couch." Casey added.

Unless you marry him tonight! I thumped my tail.

"What are you thinking, Jackie Lee? We will need to get a big bed when we get married. 5 of us in bed! Wow, that will be a cozy night." Casey pulled me to her and gave me a hug.

The guys were still putting in the alarm and it was lunch time; I was hungry. I looked at Casey.

"I know, it's lunch time. Let me ask the guys if they want some lunch, then I'll just go buy it. I think I can drive into town. It's my right ankle so I'll just be careful." Casey got up and went inside to take lunch orders. They gave Casey directions to King Arthur's Bistro Café. We jumped in the car and drove into town. Casey's phone rang. She pulled over and picked it up.

"Hello?" Casey answered.

"Casey, it's Peter."

"Hi Honey, what time will you be here?"

"I'm driving to the airport with the dogs right now, we fly out in an hour. It's a 4-hour flight as you know; then I decided to fly into Tintagel, that's another hour from London. It's noon now; we will be there at 7 tonight. Do you feel well enough to pick me up Honey or should I get another car?" Peter asked.

Casey had the phone on speaker.

"Jackie Lee and I will pick you up, see you then; have a safe flight Peter."

"I will, you be safe Casey. Take care of her Jackie Lee." Peter laughed when I woofed.

He hung up and we continued on our way.

Leaving the Café with bags of food we climbed back into the car and drove home.

Getting out of the car, Casey chuckled. I cocked my head looking at her.

"I just got a vision of three German Shepherds in the Mini. It won't work. I need to see if we can trade it in for something bigger. I love driving it, but it is not practical." She was laughing as we walked into the cottage.

I had to agree, none of us wanted to be left behind, so a bigger car it was.

The alarm was in, lunch was over. Casey and I were shown how to turn on the alarm and how to turn it off, exactly where the sensors were, etc.

Casey called the airport in Tintagel and found out that there was a car rental place there and we could trade in the Mini Cooper.

We spent the afternoon going through more of the letters, they were from Ministers of States, Iran, Iraq, and Germany. Very odd, then there were love letters to Irene, Grandpa Lane's first wife. They were really mushy, Casey blushed.

"I think we'll put these away." She laughed getting up. "It's time to get ready. TO GO pick up our family, Jackie Lee! I love the sound of that."

Casey bathed, then put on a pretty maroon dress, that was below her knees, and she put on some slip-on shoes. Then she wrapped her ankle again.

Before leaving she turned on the alarm and locked the doors. I ran around the house to see that no one was there and then jumped into the car with Casey for our final Mini ride. She had the top down and it was fun letting the wind whip my fur and ears. Casey had glasses on me so my eyes were protected.

We were a bit early, but she wanted to trade in the car. We got there and ended trading it for a Dodge Journey. It wasn't as cute, but it was roomy. All of us would be able to fit in here! I was getting really excited for the plane to land. I had missed TJ, Captain, and Peter too, more than I thought I would. Casey and I got out of the rental car and we waited. Suddenly we saw the plane coming in for a landing. Not long now! Then the plane stopped, the door opened and Peter came out of the plane first with T.J. then Captain behind him. Then the strangest thing happened!

4

BARON CAME OUT, next was Andre, then Marge and the Princess of Liechtenstein, Alexandria.

Peter ran over to Casey with a big grin on his face.

"Hi Sweetheart!" Peter grabbed Casey giving her a big kiss and swung her around.

I greeted T.J. and Captain! I was so happy to see them! I greeted everyone else again as I ran around after Peter and Casey.

Casey was laughing, "What's going on? Why is everyone here?"

Before he could answer a Limousine pulled up and stopped by our Dodge. They got out and hugged Casey and talked nonstop. Everyone was so happy.

"Casey, we are getting married, you said yes, and I'm not about to let you get away from me. We have rooms booked at a hotel near here, so we will go there first and get settled. Then we can swing by the cottage and get what you need. Tonight, we are having a dinner with everyone, tomorrow, where is he?" Peter looked around. "Oh, come here Father Dave, let me introduce you to Casey." Peter looked at Casey, "Father will marry us on the cliffs overlooking a magnificent view of Cornwall." Father approached and Peter introduced him to Casey.

"Father, this is Casey." Peter shook his hand.

"Hello Casey, I must say Peter is marrying a beautiful young lady." Father shook Casey's hand.

"Thank you, Father are you Alexandria's Priest?"

"Yes, I am, Peter got your birth certificate and all other documents to my office last week. I'm honored to come here and marry you to Peter."

Casey smiled, "I'm honored to have you do it."

"Come everyone, in the limo!" Alexandria called.

"Alexandria, Casey and I will follow you

with the dogs."

"OK Peter, we will see you there." Alexandria stepped inside the limo and everyone followed.

We drove out of Tintagel about 45 minutes into the little fishing Port of Padstow; which was on the northwest coast of Cornwall; then the limo pulled up to The Metropole Hotel. It was grand looking, looming on the top of the estuary, with stunning views.

We walked into the lobby only to find that Prince Adam Liechtenstein was waiting for his beautiful wife and all of us.

"Peter this is soooo exciting! We need to get your things in your room, then go to the cottage and get back to get ready for a memorable evening." Casey was pretty excited, I can't remember seeing her this happy for a long time, and that made me happy.

Yippee, Peter got his room, then came back with a set of keys for Casey's room and handed them to her.

"I'm ready, let's roll out kids." Peter took Casey's hand and ushered all of us out of the lobby. The attendant had our car waiting, so Peter tipped him and we climbed in.

Casey was right T.J., we would have been a funny site in the Mini we rented!

T.J. and Captain got a howl out of that.

"Listen to them Peter, ha-ha, we had better tire them out before we go back." Casey was laughing.

"I agree, do I turn here, Honey?" Peter didn't know where the cottage was.

"I'm sorry Peter," Casey slapped her forehead, "silly me, you haven't been here. Yes, a right here, then we are on the right about a half mile on this road. I'll tell you when to slow down."

"There it is." Casey pointed.

"Nice place." Peter pulled into the driveway.

Casey jumped out when the car stopped and let us out. I jumped out and showed the other two around. Always keeping Casey in my peripheral view. I ran up to her as she approached the door and punched in the alarm.

"I had to get this, because someone is

stalking us." Casey looked around and shuttered. "It's creepy, Peter."

"I know it is and we will get to the bottom of it after our wedding. Why don't you go get some things and I'll keep an eye on the dogs outside?"

"OK Peter, she kissed him."

"Not so fast, let's check the place over first." Peter stepped in front of Casey and walked in. "Nice place, it doesn't look like anyone has been back, does it Casey?" Peter turned to see Casey's reaction.

Casey was looking around, "No, should I bring the box full of surprises?"

"No honey, I think it's better here with the alarm, we won't be in our room much the next few days." Peter was right so Casey agreed.

We were there about an hour, when Peter whistled and we ran back to the car. I checked out the whole property and didn't smell anyone strange, so I didn't think the burglars had come back, yet. However, I was sure we hadn't seen the last of them.

Driving back, Casey and Peter were

talking about what had been going on. "Peter, I meant to call that Historian and it slipped my mind to do it!"

"That's fine, honey, you have had a lot of things to digest lately. I want to do this with you, after the wedding." Peter smiled at Casey, "You knew I'd say that, right?"

"You mean the part about, after the wedding?" she laughed.

"Yes, I know I sound like a broken record; however, I'm not letting this chance get away from me." Peter grinned at Casey.

"Keep your eyes on the road mister." Casey was amused.

"Yes ma'am!" Peter looked straight ahead.

Our family was going to be adventurous even when someone wasn't after us, or we were being blown out of a plane. We sure have had years of entertainment at our expense. Poor Steve, I always thought we'd end up with him. He was more serious than Peter, he was a Police Chief now and I guess that would give a person a different take on the world. Peter on the other hand, had owned a hotel on a peaceful island.

Sandy Island was a magical island in the Caribbean, Peter owned part of the island and the hotel. We could always call that home. I think Casey should sell the place in Coeur d'Alene, we had this place and Peter's condo in St. Moritz, Switzerland. I looked up, T.J. had nudged me, we were back at the hotel. Let the fun begin!

Woof!! I cried out in happiness, wagging my tail.

Casey turned around and looked at me. "I know it's exciting Jackie Lee, but you be a good boy while we're here, that goes for all three of you." She looked at us seriously.

I gave her my paw. You can count on me to be good and the others will too, Casey.

Peter stopped in front and the valet took Peter's keys after we unloaded. Peter told us we were on the third floor. We took the elevator up; our rooms were connecting. Peter took Casey's bag into our room, she was still limping, Peter didn't want her to hurt her ankle any more than it already was. He then went over and unlocked the adjoining door to his room.

"Let me go into my room and unlock this door from my side. Then I want to unwrap your ankle and have a look at it Casey." Peter helped her into a chair.

He left T.J. and Casey then went out and in a few minutes, he was back from inside his room. T.J, bounced through the joining door, I ran after him. Both rooms were nice, neither of them had a deck but full-length windows gave a clear view of the water. We had a king size bed, with a blue comforter, two brown leather recliners in front of the window with a table in between them, and chandeliers overhead. The bathroom was amazing, marble floors, a JACUZZI!!!!! Yippee!!! I loved Jacuzzi's, Casey only let me in until the water warmed up and not for long. It felt good on my body and I wanted a bath, if she didn't get around to it, I'd take one myself. He he.

Peter had Casey's bandage off, he inspected her ankle, "How's that Honey?" he asked Casey.

She winced, "It's sore."

"I think it's just a bruise but we should have it looked at Casey." Peter looked at her waiting for a response.

"After the wedding, Peter!" Casey laughed.

"Now you're sounding like me." Peter reached up and kissed her. "I can't wait to marry you!"

"It's going to be amazing Peter, amazing." Casey leaned back into the chair.

Peter stood up and placing his hands on each side of her chair asked, "Would my lady like a glass of wine?"

Casey opened her eyes, "That would be lovely kind sir. Shall we order dinner for the crew too?"

"My thoughts exactly, let me open the wine and place a dinner order in for the kids, then we can get ready to go down for our dinner." Peter walked into his room and came back a minute later with two glasses of chilled wine. He placed his on the table and handed Casey hers. Then he walked over to the phone and ordered for us. I couldn't believe what he ordered, so I kept quiet and decided to wait to see if it was true. I didn't want myself to be disappointed.

"Casey, we can keep these rooms and have the wedding breakfast here or we can move into the bridal suite tomorrow night. With the dogs, I really think we should take it. It's on the first floor, there is a deck and easy access onto the lawns, it overlooks the water too and its part of the package. What do you want to do?" Peter didn't have to wait long.

"Absolutely! Peter I'm so impressed! I need a wedding dress though! I forgot!" Casey looked worried.

Peter got up and looked at Casey, "Wait here." He walked into the other room and came back with a box. Then placed it on the bed.

"Come here and have a look Casey." Peter helped her up and walked her over to the package.

Casey looked at Peter in wonder.

"Open it!" he said.

Casey took the top off and gasped! "Peter!" She picked it up and put it in front of her. "It's perfect! I love it!"

"I'm so pleased! Alexandria helped me pick it out from her dressmaker. Do you want to go try it on?" Peter asked. "I'll go next door, because there is room service and dinner for doggies!"

"Yes, let me freshen up, I'll be over when I'm done." Casey kissed him, then picked up the dress and hurried into the bathroom.

I went next door to help Peter answer the door.

He didn't need help he told me.

The server brought in a cart of steaming food and three dishes. Yum.

Peter tipped her, then started dishing out the food.... there was a big steak for each of us, HOT DOG! Then mashed potatoes, peas, carrots, broccoli and whatever Peter just put on it.... yum, yogurt!

I savored every bite.

Casey came into the room before I finished.

"Wow! Peter really took care of you guys tonight. All of you had better thank him." Casey laughed.

I wagged my tail as I scarfed the last morsel up.

"Casey, you look beautiful." Peter walked over and hugged her. How's your ankle?"

"I left off the bandage and put this blue dress on, you like it?" she asked coyly.

"I love it and the person wearing it too. The dogs are done, they won't need to go out for a bit and our dinner is starting. Why don't we go down and before dessert I'll come up and take them out?" Peter took Casey's arm. She had a light black silk wrap on over her shoulders.

"A grand plan, let us depart."

"Jackie Lee, T.J. and Captain, we will be back. Peter put a Lassie movie on for all of you, enjoy it." With that they departed.

I went over and leaned against the bed watching the movie. T.J. did too and Captain jumped on the bed and fell asleep.

The door opened and shocked all of us!

5

I JUMPED UP and lunged, T.J. was right after me! Captain hid under the bed. It was the guy that was digging in the garden! He pointed a gun at us and told us to stand down.

I went for his leg and knocked him over, the cart with the empty food trays fell over making a horrid clatter.

T.J. bit his arm holding the gun, he dropped it.

Someone in the hallway screamed for help. Hotel security rushed in and grabbed the guy, Peter was behind them.

"What's going on?" Peter demanded to know.

"This guy broke into your room and must have tried to rob you, but your dogs took him down. He's a known criminal and will work for anyone. So, he's robbing you for himself or someone else. We need to take him down to the police station; I'll have them contact you if they find out anything." The guard said.

"Do you know his name?" Peter asked.

"He has many names; his real name no one knows. We notified the hotel to call room service; they will come clean up this mess." The guard had him in cuffs and took him past Peter; he glared at Peter as he was being drug off.

"Come on, you dogs come with me, the party is on the lawn and you're invited. I was just coming to get you. The maids have a huge mess to clean up anyway. Where's Captain? Captain?" Peter called, then looked under the bed. "Come out buddy, it's OK." Peter reached underneath the bed and took Captain's collar urging him out.

Peter put Captain on a leash, then T.J. and I followed them down to dinner.

"Peter what happened? Why were you so long? I was getting worried." Casey said as she leaned over and petted Captain.

"A guy broke into my room, but Jackie Lee and T.J. nailed the guy. Hotel Security took him down to the police station. They said basically he was a thug for hire." Peter sat down next to Casey.

"Well, if that doesn't amaze me. Let's try to forget it tonight, until...." Casey was interrupted.

Peter said, "After the wedding."

"Yes, that's it." Casey laughed.

The evening passed by quickly with no more interruptions.

That night I slept next to Casey, she was awake for a long time. I know she was making the right decision. It was so nice of our new friends to take time out of their lives and come to Cornwall for a wedding. Plus, it helped give us some fun before we pursued the trail of Casey's grandfather being a SPY!

I finally fell asleep.....We were in South America someplace, it was humid. Casey and I were in an estate and the breeze was blowing through the white lace curtains. Two teenage children were sitting around a dinner table with Casey's grandfather and his first wife, Margaretta, apparently, because that is what he called her. They didn't see us and it was strange.

They were talking about the kid's school work, when a knock at the door stopped them.

"Kids! Go to your rooms and lock the doors." He rose from the table and turned towards Margaretta. "You know what to do if something happens."

She didn't say anything but nodded her head yes. After he went to the door, she went to check on her kids.

The conversation at the door was quick. It was an informant apparently. He had information for James Lane, James shut the door and locked it. Then he called Margaretta and the kids. When they sat at the table, he told them to resume eating.

Then he said. "The time has come, the trail is hot again, it's going to get dangerous. I need for you to pack your things. You will fly out of here tomorrow, and go back to England."

He looked at the kids, "Your mother will fill you in, it's best you don't know more." He shook his head. "It's just too dangerous..."

The next morning, he sent them off on a small aircraft to connect to a larger one for the flight back to England. He didn't know that would be the last time he would see his beloved Margaretta.

"Jackie Lee, buddy...you're kicking me, wake up." Casey was gently shaking me to stop running.

I woke up, Casey I was on the case! You woke me, now I don't know where he went.

"How about a drink of water?" Casey got out of bed and grabbed her water, she took a drink then let me finish it.

Thanks, chasing criminals is thirsty business.

I fell back to sleep and the dream returned......

6

WEDDING DAY!!! I barked to my buddies, T.J. and Captain, as soon as Casey opened our connecting doors.

Everyone was excited.

"Casey, let's have a light breakfast. I already called room service, and then I will leave you alone to get ready. Alexandria and Marge will be here to help you get ready. How did you sleep last night?" Peter kissed Casey on her forehead.

"Pretty good, except Jackie Lee was having some vivid dreams."

The door was being knocked on.

"There's room service Peter."

Peter turned to go back to his door.

"Good, I'll be right back."

"Who is it?" Peter asked the person knocking.

I think that was pretty smart of him, after the activity we have had with burglars lately.

Peter answered the door convinced it was room service and wheeled the food cart over to his table. All of us went over and had breakfast. I was excited to see the kind of food Peter had ordered for us today. Last night rocked!!

When breakfast was done I went over with Casey, she needed me, I could tell.

Peter closed his door to get ready and go down to see how things were progressing. This was going to be such a fun day......

Alexandria and Marge arrived together, they had their dresses over their arms and other things that were needed.

Casey was finally in her dress, she looked beautiful, but she was stunning in anything she wore. The other women were dressed in mauve silk gowns with blue flowers, down to their ankles. Casey had on a pretty snow-white wedding dress, it had straps and no sleeves, the dress was ankle length and the vale flowed down to the floor. The time arrived. We left the room and made it out to the garden. The garden was overlooking the water on a high cliff. The little wedding party was down there waiting for the girls. T.J. and Captain had on stylish tie collars, Peter slipped one on me too. Baron walked Casey down the aisle, Casey had tears in her eyes.

I knew she was making the right decision, all of us were a team and it made no sense to wander the world solving crimes and mysteries if we weren't a real family. I know that's why it was so important to Peter to tie the knot with Casey. T.J. and I had discussed this many times.

Casey didn't run away and neither did Peter. It was a quick wedding.

The 'I Do's' were said and everyone cheered!!!! Now we could all stay in the same room!!! We would need a really big bed, I slept with Casey too.

The reception went until about 8 PM. Stories were swapped about the adventure we just had in St. Moritz. Alexandria and Adam were flying to Amsterdam in the morning, so we said our goodbyes to them and promised to keep in touch. They were family now. Marge was going to stay with Baron, Scott and Andre; they planned on touring Cornwall and would be in touch in a couple of days.

The hotel had moved our belongings down to the bridal suite, Casey and Peter said goodnight to our friends and we went in search of our new room and new life.

The room was on the ground floor and opened up to the beach. It was a bit of a hike down to the water, but in the morning, we could go down there and at least walk the beach.

T.J., Captain and I all piled in bed with Casey and Peter, there was little wiggle room. I was on Casey's feet, T.J. was on Peter's and Captain was in between them. All of us were so exhausted that we fell quickly to sleep.

It must have been early morning, I heard a noise outside our room on the patio. I jumped off the bed and looked through the blinds.

A man I didn't recognize was trying to open the sliding door!

7

I BARKED AND lunged at him, Peter grabbed a Glock from his suitcase and was right behind me. It came in mighty handy tonight.

"Stay Jackie Lee; Honey, call security!" Peter opened the door as the guy took off.

"Coward!" Peter shouted angrily and then turned back towards the room.

"Peter, I called them, they're circling the hotel looking for this guy. What do these guys want?" Casey was bewildered so early in the morning.

"Casey, I'm wondering the same thing, did you find something in that box worth stealing?"

"OHH, the map!" Casey ran over to her bag and opened it. "Whew! It's still here."

"Pull it out, Honey, and let's have a look." Peter cleared off the table and pulled out a chair for Casey to sit in.

Casey brought the map over and spread it open on the table.

"Look, it's a map, someplace in Brazil! There are x's on certain spots. What does it mean? My grandfather was down there after the war chasing war criminals, at least that's what Aunt Claire thought. Peter! We forgot to invite her to our wedding!" Casey was horrified!

"One thing at a time, Aunt Claire can't travel anymore, that is what you told me, we will go visit her and have a celebration with her. Ok?"

Casey shook her head up and down, agreeing.

"Next, if your grandfather was onto something but never caught the person....."Peter trailed off.

"That person could still be prosecuted! Or the relatives could be trying to hide something. I'm a threat!" Casey sighed, she looked troubled.

Peter put his hand over hers. "We could walk away and go to Sandy Island or Coeur d'Alene?"

"I know we could, but I love this cottage and I want to find out more about my grandfather." Casey answered.

"Then that's what we'll do, fly with it, we are in search of the truth!" Peter slammed his hand on the table, "I'm in, are you in Jackie Lee, T.J. and Captain?"

I high fived Peter, T.J. barked and Captain thumped his tail.

"Well, I am way too wound up to go back to sleep, how about you Peter?"

"I'm with you, why don't we get changed and take the dogs down to the water, daylight is upon us, we can watch the sun rise." Peter hugged Casey.

"Very romantic, let's get going." Casey slipped out of Peter's arms and grabbed some clothes from her suitcase.

"I'll be right out." Casey slipped into the bathroom.

"OK, we will be out here waiting." Peter grabbed some of his clothes and changed, then opened up the patio doors and let us out.

I played with T.J. and Captain until Casey was ready. Finally, she came outside.

"Grab my hand love, and I'll help you down this hill." Peter stretched out his hand.

Casey took it and let Peter help her. It was slippery with the morning dew. We got down to the beach, no one was there. We walked to the end of the beach, and when we started back the sky was reddening from a beautiful sunrise. The sand was white, and felt so good on my feet. Casey took her shoes off; she must have agreed with me.

We got back to our part of the beach and Casey and Peter found a log to sit on. We sat by them and watched the sun rise, it was beautiful in this spot. I wish we could stay here forever.......

Casey and Peter planned the day for us.

When we got back to the room, a big breakfast was sitting on a cart with enough food for all of us!!

After eating, we loaded our stuff in the SUV and Peter drove us back to our English cottage. We were shocked when we arrived.

"Good thing for the security, Casey. Look! The whole garden has been turned over!"

Casey jumped out of the SUV and I bounded after her.

Yep, someone dug the garden up and threw the dirt everywhere! I knew they were looking for the chest Casey found and the contents of it too.

"It's OK! I will use this dirt to fill the raised garden beds I'm going to build." Peter looked up at Casey grinning.

"Great attitude, Dear." Casey kissed his head. "Let's check the cottage."

Peter stood up and followed Casey to the front door. She put in the alarm code and unlocked the door.

Stepping inside, Casey went into the bedroom and pulled the chest out, then carried it into the living room and sat it down on the desk. Peter walked over and looked inside.

"These photos are amazing; I'm sure Aunt Claire would love them." Peter was amazed.

Casey said, "I think she would too."

"Besides the map, there doesn't seem to be anything in here of value to robbers. What do you say we load up the SUV and drive to see Aunt Claire tomorrow? I want to go look in the attic too, I think we can clean that up and make a nice bedroom out of it." Peter thought for a minute.

"That's a wonderful idea on both accounts Peter! Come'on, let's go look at the attic; I'll put this chest under the desk, so it isn't visible from outside."

Casey slipped it under the desk and ran up the stairs after Peter.

"Casey, look! THE VIEW OF THE SEA!!! Let me start going through these things left in the attic, let's order some furniture for up here too. A king bed for sure with these guys. We need to be able to roll over in the night." He laughed, "true?"

"Ha, yes, I agree. There are Christmas decorations, some books and old clothes in the boxes I opened. We can donate everything to charity, except the Christmas decorations, we need to get a storage unit for some things." Casey was opening boxes as she talked.

"Why don't you let me load these things in the SUV; can you find a place for me to take it?" Peter asked, then continued, "We soon need to get online and order what furniture you want for up here. I can store the decorations in the bedroom downstairs until I build a storage shed out back."

'I'll get right on it." Casey went downstairs and found a charity nearby.

Peter came in after he put the last load in the SUV.

Casey handed him the address, "It's just a 1 kilometer down the road. Do you want me to go with you or stay and shop online?" Asked Casey.

"Why don't you stay. I'll take Captain, you keep T.J. and Jackie Lee here to guard you from our unwanted friends. We'll be right back." Peter leaned over and kissed her.

"I'll get to work; the views up there are stunning in the attic. I'm so glad Aunt Claire kept this place for her half-brother's family. She must have had the faith she would find him or his family someday."

"So am I, we won't want to spend too many winters here, in Cornwall though. We have other options for harsh winters." Peter wasn't kidding, too many other options.

"Let's talk about that too, Peter. We don't need the house in America, I could get a lot for the home I bought last year. It's beautiful and since we won't be living there full time, it's a waste to keep it. Let me call the realtor I bought it from. It's furnished, but I can sell the furniture to whomever buys it, my personal effects are minimal. I can hire someone to box them up and send them over, like my clothes. Jackie Lee has always slept with me, so he won't miss his dog bowls and they have all the toys in the world now; plus, beaches for entertainment. I've thought long and hard on this, Honey."

"Casey, if that's what you want to do, I don't have any objection to your decision, love. I'll hurry back, lock the front door after us." Peter kissed her and left with Captain.

"Good boys," Casey was talking to T.J. and me, "We can do a lot of fun stuff with that money from the house. We can fix this one up, it's so cute, I love this cottage."

Woof! Woof! I barked.

GRRRR! T.J. barred his teeth.

We both looked at the kitchen door. There was a noise out back.

"What is it boys?" Casey grabbed a broom, which was by the back door, and pushed the kitchen curtains back a bit and froze!

8

"WHAT DO THEY think they are doing?" Casey opened the back door and shouted at the two men.

"STOP DIGGING! THIS IS MY HOUSE!"
They stopped what they were doing and looked at her. These were two men we had never before seen.

"Hey lady, sorry. We were hired to find something on this property." The man with the jean jacket said. They were both about 30 years old and lean.

"Who hired you?" Casey asked.

"We didn't meet anyone, it was a phone call, and then we received a ton of cash to locate a chest. We both thought this house belonged to the guy that called us, wc're Private Investigators. The other guy that had on boots and a green T-shirt removed his gloves and reached into his pocket.

"Here's our business card." He offered it to Casey; she stepped out of the house and approached the men. Of course, T.J. and I accompanied her, sticking to her like glue.

Casey took the card and read it. Then she stuck out her hand, "I'm Casey and this is T.J. and Jackie Lee."

"You're American!" The man with the jean jacket said.

"Yes, this was my grandparent's home. I've just inherited it. We have been robbed, broken into and our property dug up. I don't understand what is going on?" Casey told them.

The men picked up their shovels, "We'll fill the hole back in and clean up this mess, I'm Jack." The jean jacket guy said. "This is my brother Robert. We promise to get to the bottom of this, the guy is supposed to call us back tonight."

"It's getting frightening." Casey said, "I just got married and they tried to break into our room in the hotel too!"

"We're sorry, write your number down for us and we can tell you what we find out when the guy contacts us again." Robert said.

"Alright, I'll be right back." Casey and I went back into the house, T.J. stayed by the kitchen door watching them.

"Jackie Lee, help me find some paper." I took off and went into the bedroom. Casey's suitcase was open and I grabbed a writing tablet out of it, then took it back to her in the kitchen.

"Thanks buddy." She kissed my nose.

I wagged my tail and watched her scribble some information on a sheet of paper from the tablet.

Casey ripped it off the pad and walked back outside. The men were done and things were picked up.

"Here," Casey handed them her information.

"Where is your car?" Casey asked.

"We parked down the street in the park and walked over." Jack said.

"You said the man should contact you tonight?"

Casey asked.

"Yes, we will be in touch, do you mind if we use your driveway to walk off your property?" Robert asked.

"No, I don't mind, be my guest." Casey said as we followed them around to the front of our house.

Peter pulled up as we approached the driveway.

He quickly got out of the SUV and walked over to talk to the men.

"Hi, Peter, this is Robert and Jack. They are
Private Investigators and they were anonymously hired to find a buried treasure on our property." Casey looked at Peter.

Peter shook their hands, "We need to find out what's going on. If you can shed some light on this matter, please let us know."

"I have their card and they have our information, Peter." Casey said.

"Good, then I will say goodbye, Casey and I have a lot to do."

"Goodbye," both men said and walked out onto the road.

Peter turned to Casey, "This is a very popular place." He put his arm around her, "Come see what I bought."

"What did you buy?" Casey asked.

They walked over to the SUV, Peter let Captain out and he showed us what he bought.

"Wood for a garden bed, and a wonderful king futon for us to sleep on until our new furniture arrives." Peter was pretty happy.

"The futon is a great idea! Let's get this stuff out of here. I'll help." Casey grabbed the futon and Peter grabbed the other end. They carried it into the house and took it up to the attic.

"Let's put it under the window by the side of the house, so we can look out of the windows towards the back of the house and the sea." Peter said.

"Yes, ohhh, this is nice. I'll grab some sheets out of the pantry and the blankets off the bed downstairs." Casey took off to make the futon cozy.

"I'll dump the wood along the side of the house Casey while you do that." Peter said as he followed her out of the room.

"Great, I'll turn on the laptop and look for furniture when I finish." Casey said.

"I ordered a pizza for us and bought some cooked chicken and veggies for the boys." Peter added.

"Fantastic! No cooking saves time." Then Casey and Peter went their separate ways.

We had been fed, Casey and Peter were eating Pizza and shopping online.

"That's the last of furniture we need. The bed, night stands and dressers will be here in a week. The bedding will arrive tomorrow. How about a nice hike tomorrow while we wait for Robert and Jack to get back to us? My ankle is feeling better." Casey asked.

"If you're sure, I like that train of thought, and then maybe you can help me build the two garden beds?" Peter asked.

"Yesss, I can do that, but I'm not sure planting anything right now is wise. What if we have to go to Brazil?" Casey asked.

"I thought of that; it will be a perfect time to put in some squash when we are done with Brazil, if we go." Peter added.

Casey and Peter grabbed some balls for us, some water and then we took off out the kitchen door for the beach.

I was in such a hurry, I missed whether Casey or Peter set the alarm.

The tide was out and we played ball until we couldn't run anymore. Casey and Peter were looking pretty tired too. So, they called time-up for play and we took the trail back to the house.

"Peter, I didn't set the alarm, did you?" Casey asked him.

"Yes, dear, I did, or I think I did." Peter hurried ahead of us.

Casey ran after him and I was hot on her trail, even though I was exhausted.

Jack and Robert were waiting for us by the kitchen door.

"Hi Casey and Peter," Jack walked up to us.

"Hi," Robert said.

"Hi guys, what's up? Did you get a call from the person that hired you?" Peter asked.

"Hi," Casey said as she walked up and stood by Peter, waiting for an explanation.

"Yes, we did. The guy called, he was disguising his voice again. It was just all too obvious that he was up to something. We told him that there was nothing buried around the house. Then we asked him, what was it he really wanted to find?" Robert paused.

Jack picked up where Robert left off, "He was evasive. We asked for a meeting with him, again he put us off. So, we told him we were done. That made him change his tune. He said he was looking for a map or list, that he must have it, before someone else did."

"This made us think, there are several different people wanting the same thing. The value of the map or list just got higher." Robert added.

Both of them finished each other's sentences, they must be twins! I thought.

"We decided to talk to you first. We don't plan on working for this guy. We asked him where we could return his money? He told us, we couldn't. We accepted the work and money, he was holding us accountable to finish the job." Jack said.

Robert added, "We think you must have the missing link and that it must relate to this house, your relatives or something. We told him nothing about meeting you. If we tell him we met you, he will think you have some knowledge of what he is seeking."

"What if he is the only one searching? He could have hired all of these other men that have been trying to break in and search our house. Don't you think that makes sense?" Peter put his arm around Casey. "What have you two decided to do? We feel there is too much suspicious activity for this to be nothing or a random thing. Casey and Jackie Lee were almost killed a few days ago, when a truck tried to run them over."

The men were thoughtful, then Robert spoke, "We think we should play along with him right now, not tell him anything. That way we can maybe know what he is thinking. We would like to work with you."

"Only if out of curiosity, we aren't seeking payment, but we feel we could help each other." Jack looked at his brother. Robert nodded in agreement.

Peter looked at Casey, then at Jack and Robert. "Let Casey and I have a talk, can you wait out here, we'll take the dogs in and then be right out to tell you our thoughts."

"Sure, we can't go back to the office with nothing or the guy will be suspicious. He told us that at 6 tonight someone would be by our office to pick up what he wanted." Robert said.

"We'll be right back, excuse us." Peter unlocked the door, told us to go inside and Casey followed us through the door.

"What idea do you have Peter?"

"Casey, let's give them the chest. You have the map, let's take out the pictures. We've gone through the chest, there isn't anything else."

"Wait! I have an idea! Follow me." Casey ran into the living room and pulled the case out from under the desk. She sat on the floor with the chest in front of her. Peter sat down next to her. Casey opened the chest. She pulled out the photos of her family and then took out the other items, a rosary, a prayer book, letters and a few other things too. Then she got up and took some scissors out of the desk.

"What are doing?" Peter asked.

Casey said nothing but smiled and raised her eyebrows, her look said it all. I know something you don't. She took the scissors and started cutting the fabric around the bottom of the chest. She pulled back the cloth, so the chest bottom could be seen.

"Look!" Casey said.

"I see! Lucky guess or intuition?" Peter asked.

"A bit of both." Casey answered.

9

CASEY REACHED INSIDE and using the scissors, took the cover off the cubby hole. Inside was an envelope. Casey carefully pulled it out.

"Peter, here, can you open it? I'm too nervous to do it."

"Sure," Peter took it carefully out of Casey's hands. He opened the envelope and pulled out a paper. He unfolded the paper and put it flat on the floor, so Casey could follow along.

"Peter, there's names, places, dates, items." Casey whispered.

"I know. Let's put the rosary in the hole." Peter said as he picked up the rosary. Then he laid the fabric back down. "Is that ok, or do you want to keep it?"

"It's ok, I have plenty of rosaries. What else should we put back inside?" Casey asked.

The letters and photos need to go to Aunt Claire. Let's put the gloves and prayer book, some of these small trinkets, unless you want anything?" Peter asked.

Casey picked up the prayer book and opened it. "There's writing in here, I'd like to hang onto it Peter."

"That's fine, let me put some other things back in. Why don't you take this envelope and place it with the map? We need to analyze them carefully when we have time, like tonight. I'll take the chest out to the guys. Do we want to team up with them?" Peter asked.

"Let's decide after we study everything. It might be a good time to take this and visit Aunt Claire. Perhaps she can enlighten us a bit?"

"I agree, Casey. Join me outside after you take this stuff into the other room, Honey." Peter reached over and kissed Casey. Then he got up and picked up the chest. I followed him back outside, T.J. was asleep, so he stayed in his comfy spot by the couch; Captain followed Casey into the bedroom.

Peter went out the kitchen door. "Sorry it took so long, here's the chest that was buried. Casey needed some personal things out of it for her Aunt. Everything else is in here just as we found it." Peter handed over the chest to Robert.

"This is fantastic! Now we've earned our keep. I would still like to know who this guy is and what he wants."

"Me too," Jack added, but we don't want to be obligated to him in anyway, so I say good riddance after this."

"I hope so for your safety. Let us know how this goes?" Peter asked.

"Will do," Robert looked at his watch, "We need to hurry, it's after 5 now!"

"OK, talk to you guys later then?" Peter asked.

"Yes, thank you Peter and thank Casey too." Jack shook Peter's hand. Then they walked off to the front of the house and their car.

Casey came out the back door, "I missed them?"

"Yes, Honey, they just left, I asked them to be in touch."

"Peter how did it go when you handed them the chest?"

"They were relieved, it's the right thing to do. Maybe this guy will leave us alone, when he sees there's nothing in the chest." Peter said.

"Unless the man thinks we took whatever it is he is looking for." Casey added.

"There's that too, we'll worry about it when it happens. We still need to be on watch, more than ever now. Let's go inside and feed everyone and find some food for us." Peter kicked off his shoes outside the door, and hugged Casey. "Let's have some fun tonight and study the list." Peter smiled.

"My kind of fun, Peter." Casey grabbed our dinner bowls and Peter helped her feed us. Then Peter took out some steaks and threw them on the grill outside of the kitchen door.

"Casey, we need to build a deck back here, I think maybe with glass windows that can open in summer and keep closed to warm us in the winter. Then I think a hot tub would do the trick." Peter flipped the steaks, Casey handed him a glass of chilled Chardonnay." Thank you,

Sweetie." Peter took the glass from her hands and took a sip.

"You're welcome for the wine and that's a splendid idea My Dear! When will we have time for all of these ideas?" Casey smiled sweetly.

"I'll call around for some contractor's tomorrow." Peter tossed the steaks on a platter, and grabbed his wine glass. "Will you open the door, please?"

"Sure." Casey held the door open for Peter and we followed him inside.

Peter put the steaks on the plates Casey had out with a salad on each one and a baked potato too.

They carried their food into the living room and placed the food on the coffee table in front of the couch. While Casey was eating she had her laptop out and was googling Brazil and what happened there right after WW ll.

"Peter, listen to this. I found an article on the History A&E Television Network.

How South America became a Nazi Haven.

.....The German legal team that examined South American files in 2012 told the Daily Mail that most Nazis who entered did so using forged Red Cross passports, including 800 SS members to Argentina alone. Many of the Nazis who escaped to South America were never brought to justice.

Following the war, the U.S. Counter-Intelligence Corps recruited Klaus Barbie----the Gestapo chief in Lyon, France, who played a role in the deaths of thousands of French Jews and members of the French Resistance----as an agent to assist with anti-Communist efforts. He was smuggled to Bolivia, where he continued his spy work and instructed the military on how to torture and interrogate political opponents.

"Then it goes on to the fact that he was one of the Nazis who fled South America, but the Israeli court convicted him and he was executed in 1962.

http://www.history.com/news/how-south-america-became-a-nazi-haven

"Casey, where did you put that list and map? Let's see if we can make any sense out of it."

"It's in the bottom of my suitcase Honey. I'll clean up while you get it."

"OK." Peter got up and went in search of the secrets Casey's grandpa left behind.

Casey grabbed the plates and tossed all of the dishes, including ours into the dishwasher.

When we got back to the living room, I go everywhere Casey goes, Peter had the paperwork out of the envelope and was spreading it out on the coffee table. Casey sat down next to Peter.

"Look Casey! This has a list of ODESSA members!" Peter glanced over the list.

"Some are crossed off, here's one that isn't but has stars by it." Casey stated. "What is ODESSA?"

"I don't know; can you google it?" Peter asked as he read further down the page.

"Yes, here it is," Casey read what she had found.

"It was the "Organization of Former SS Members." It would only help members of the SS or Schutz Staffel (Protection Corps), which was the elite structure of the Nazi Party and Hitler's bodyguards."

"The name of that man is Priebke, he would be, let's see," Casey used the calculator on her phone, "He would be 90 now. On this website, I just found he was never caught and it is believed his son still lives in Peru. I bet his son moved after this article came out for his own safety." Casey added.

"I would think you're right. Do you think his son or a relative of his is the one wanting all of this information to have it destroyed?" Peter asked.

"It wouldn't surprise me if it was, Peter." Casey looked at him. Let's look at that map again."

Peter took the map out.

"See if you can find this Priebke on the map, Peter. I'll keep searching on the internet."

"Yikes! Listen to this!"

SS Captain Erich Priebke was discovered to be living in Bariloche, Argentina during the 1990's. Priebke was accused of ordering the massacre of 335 Italians in March 1944. The killings occurred at the Ardeatine Caves in Rome, after which Priebke ordered that the entrance be blown up to bury the bodies. He was extradited to Italy and sentenced to 15 years in prison. He is now 93, the oldest Nazi prisoner in custody.

Marcelo Mackinnon

www.english.ohmynews.com

"Well, he isn't the one. It must be some other guy on the list Peter! I must have misread the information, it's the same website." Casey looked back over the website, "Yes, I misread it, I was so excited I mixed him up with this other guy, Adolf Hiermer. Casey looked to see what Peter was finding on his IPad Pro.

"You're right," Peter said. "Casey, listen to this! This is the guy!"

"Adolf Hiermer, he was the head doctor at the Mauthausen concentration camp in Austria! They think he might still live in Brazil with his daughter! Any of these people could be onto us to keep us quiet!" Peter read on.....

There are many reasons to believe Hiermer is still in South America.

"Casey, this could be the guy, or Priebke's son could be the guy. We need to be very careful. I think we should talk to Robert and Jack: they need to work with us and not get mixed up with any of these characters!"

"You're so right about this." Casey picked up her phone, "Let's call them now."

"OK, call and put the phone on speaker." Peter said.

Casey dialed and the phone rang and rang. She hung up and looked at the card. "I dialed the right number. I wonder why they didn't pick up or no voicemail picked up?" Casey looked worried.

Peter looked at his watch. "It's 7 PM, they should have had the chest picked up by now. I hope nothing happened to them."

"Should we go and check in with them?" Casey asked.

"I don't know, what do you think?" Peter asked.

"Let me try back in a bit." Casey replied.

"Let's see what else we can find and try back in an hour then." Peter put in another search on his iPad Pro.

"What???" Peter shouted! "Casey listen to this!

The evil dictator fled to Parahuay, via Argentina, before settling in a small town in the state of Mato Grosso, Brazil, according to a shocking book. Hitler is said to have used the assumed name of Adolf Leipzig and was known to 12,000 locals in Nossa Senhora do Livramento as "The Old German."

The man at the centre of the controversial claim is pictured, two years before his death in 1984, posing happily with his black girlfriend Cutinga Simoni Renee Guerreiro Dias, who wrote Hitler in Brazil-His Life and His Death, claims he was in the area looking for buried treasure using a map given to him by friends in the Vatican.

Simoni, a Brazilian Jew, refuses to accept that the Fuhrer shot himself in his Berlin bunker on

April 30, 1945. She is demanding Leipzig's remains be exhumed and his DNA be tested against living relatives of Hitler.

http://www.express.co.uk/news/weird/4 55810/The-INCREDIBLE-picture-that-proves-Adolf-Hitler-lived-to-95-with-his-Brazilian-lover

"Casey, there could be treasure buried in Brazil! That could be the reason we are targeted as well. Maybe your grandfather was looking to see where the Germans buried the valuables stolen and taken during WW ll????"

"Wow! I never ever dreamed of anything like this! Peter, we need to go see Aunt Claire, then I think we are going on a little trip to Brazil. Let me try the boys once again." Casey picked up her phone again.

"It's crazy, but exciting Casey!" Peter kept reading.......

Casey hung up, "Peter I'm worried; let's go check on them."

"Honey where is their home? We only have their office address, don't we?" Peter looked at the card, "Maybe not, they might do business out of their home or condo."

Casey dialed the second number on the card. It too just rang and rang. She put it down. "Let's clean this up and hide it. Should we take everyone or leave two dogs here to guard the house?" Casey asked.

"We have a great security system and we have new locks on the windows and doors. Let's check to make sure everything is locked up and take everyone. I saw an ice cream shop we can stop at for a treat too." Peter laughed as T.J., Captain and I all wagged our tails and barked!

We hopped into the SUV as fast as we could; the three of us were very excited for a treat. Peter drove towards town; the boys were on the other side of the village. Peter pulled into a drive thru ice cream shop!

All three of us got a bowl of vanilla ice cream with nuts, yummy!!!! Casey got her mint chip and Peter got Rocky Road. I gobbled mine up and looked longingly at Casey's.

"You ate yours' already? Ha, you can't eat our ice cream, it has bad things in it for dogs." Casey turned back around.

I knew she was right, but it doesn't hurt to try!

Peter pulled up in front of a little two-story brick building. The sign said, R & J Detective Agency.

"Casey, I bet they live upstairs." Peter got out of the car and walked up to the front door and looked inside. Then he banged on the door and it opened....

Casey came running over to Peter. "The door just opened?" she asked.

"Yes," he opened it wider and we looked around.

The place was trashed and Robert was unconscious under his desk. He had a gash on his head. Casey bent over and took his pulse. "He has a pulse." She reached for the phone and then drew back. "Peter! Don't touch anything, we don't want to mess up any prints."

"I know, I meant to remind you. Casey! Come in here." Peter shouted.

She stood up, and followed his voice, he was in the kitchen.

There was Jack, he had been shot!

10

"PETER IS HE alive?" Casey was frantic.

Peter ran over to him and grabbed a kitchen towel tying it around Jack's arm. "He's lost some blood, he's unconscious and he's bleeding from somewhere else too! Can you call the police and have them bring the EMS? He needs medical attention right away!"

"I'm calling emergency right now! What else can I do?" Casey cried out in panic.

"Honey please find some more towels?" Peter sounded stressed.

I backed up out of the kitchen and went to look at Robert.

It wasn't long and the emergency service pulled up; they rushed in to the building. The police were right behind them.

"We got your call and brought in all forces." The EMS man said, "Where are the victims?"

Casey hurriedly told them, "I'm so happy you're here! One is over there behind the desk, but the critical one is in the kitchen!"

The men moved swiftly, two went over to Robert and two went into the kitchen where Peter was.

Casey talked to the police, then they tried to take fingerprints throughout the office and kitchen. They promised to keep Casey notified of any findings.

Peter came out to Casey and me, the EMS had just taken the young men away.

"Casey, I'm thinking Aunt Claire isn't remembering her story right or that there is something bigger about this whole affair than she knows or remembers." Peter took her hand. "Let's go home."

"Peter, I think you're right. I'm calling Aunt Claire in the morning, we should call that historian too. Did I mention that to you? I found an historian on WW 2 Spies, especially MI-5 spies. I'm suspicious about Aunt Claire's memory too." Casey was following Peter out to the SUV.

"Good idea, I think we should do some more research tonight too." Peter started the engine and we drove home in silence.

Of course, T.J. and Captain had to know what happened, so I told them.

I hope nothing else happens tonight Captain. T.J. was worried.

I hope not too, but we must watch Peter and Casey and be very aware of our surroundings when out of the cottage. I was sure I was giving T.J. and Captain a clear message of how serious our situation was.

We arrived home and all of us went into the house. I felt secure because the alarm was keeping the bad people from entering. Casey reset the alarm after we had done our business outside that night, so we just had to remember to turn it off when going outside tomorrow. Casey and Peter got back on the internet and searched for a few more hours.

"Peter there is so much here on MI-5's activities before the war, during the war and after; I think we need to have Aunt Claire's version again. She is 90, I do believe she could have forgotten what's real and what she thinks is real."

"Casey, I feel the same way. We need to make sure that she stays safe." Peter looked at Casey.

"I've thought of that too. How has she remained safe all of these years?" Casey asked.

"She was inactive, now she has found you and we are stirring up the pot." Peter was using figurative language, but I understood what he meant.

"Look Peter, I found something here, it's Wikipedia, but we can check other sources too. Let me read this to you......"

Due to the spy hysteria in the 1920's, MI5 had been formed with far more resources than it actually needed to track down German Spies.

https://en.wikipedia.org/wiki/MI5

"So, before the war he could have been in Buenos Aires with your Aunt Claire and his family; looking for German spies. Brazil, Argentina, Venezuela all sympathized with the Germans during WW 1 and 2. After the war he could have been down there to look for Nazi's hiding and the treasures they stored. There is so much, and so many reasons someone is trying to stop us. I know it just makes you want to search for the truth and I don't blame you. I feel the same way, but we need to be safe and on guard. Let me call the hospital and check on the young men." Peter picked up his phone and dialed the hospital.

When he hung up he was worried.

"They aren't sure Jack is going to make it Casey. We need to go visit him tomorrow. They said if we hadn't been there he would have died right there."

"Poor Robert, poor Jack, I feel so bad about this Peter!" Casey got tears in her eyes.

"Me too, but we didn't get them into this Honey, they got themselves into it. Remember that, but we will do anything we can for them." Peter reached over and hugged Casey. "Let's go to bed and try to sleep, we have our new room upstairs! We had better go before the dogs beat us to it."

Casey laughed, "It's big enough for all of

us and our mattress will be plenty big for all of us to, I can't wait to get it. However, this is like camping and it's fun." Casey jumped up, put her computer in its case and stored it on the desk. Then she went into the kitchen and made some tea for Peter and herself. They gave us a snack as they snacked and drank their tea, then all of us went to bed.

I was sleeping so soundly, but my dreams were making me restless. Why was I dreaming about Casey and me being with her grandpa, but he doesn't see us and we see what he's doing? I think my imagination is running away with me.

I sat up, sniff, sniff, smoke, smoke somewhere!

I woke T.J. and Captain, we jumped on Peter and Casey and got them up.

Peter sprang out of bed running down the stairs so fast I couldn't keep up with him. By the time we got down the stairs, we saw what was happening.

Peter didn't turn off the alarm so it was ringing and smoke was everywhere!

11

THE SMOKE WAS out the front door, someone had placed a pile of branches by our front door and started a fire!

Peter ran out the back door around to the front grabbed the hose Casey was following him and turned it on for him. He got the fire out just as the police arrived.

"Hi Officer Harrison, we need to stop meeting like this." Peter shook the same officer's hand that we had met earlier when Robert and Jack were in trouble.

"Yes, I think there is danger all around the five of you." He said that because of Peter, Casey and the three of us all standing around him and the ashes in our front yard.

"I don't know what's going on, but perhaps you would like to meet with us tomorrow and tell us?" Officer Harrison asked.

"I'm not sure it's anything we can explain."

Said Casey, "I just inherited this house and with it old photos of my grandfather. We found that he wasn't who we thought he was, so it's a bit touchy to discuss with anyone right now. We will be sure to enlist your help when we find out what that help entails."

"Fine, but I hope we don't find any of you shot or dead." Officer Harrison filed his report and they left.

Peter looked at Casey, "It's barely light out, what time is it?"

"I don't know, but I'm going to make us some coffee. I can't go back to sleep now." Casey walked around the mess of burnt wood and into the house.

Indeed, it was 4:30 AM, Peter looked at his IPhone. "Casey, maybe a catnap this afternoon then, we have tons of important work to accomplish today and I don't think it's going to be an early night. I don't want you to get sick on me when I'm still recovering. How is your ankle feeling right now? You said it was better but we have been active and you haven't complained about it."

"It hurts some, but it's getting better, I haven't thought of it, there's too much going on." Peter gave her a cup of coffee. She took a sip, "Let's go lay down for an hour then after we drink this."

"Good idea, I'm not even going to drink coffee right now, neither should you." Peter took the cup from Casey's hands.

"You're right, as always, I'm nervous enough already." Casey put her arms around Peter's neck and buried her face in his chest.

"Shh, it's ok, Sweetie, let's take everyone up and have a rest." Peter picked Casey up and carried her upstairs, with me trailing behind them. T.J. and Captain followed us up the stairs too.

Casey fell right to sleep, so I shut my eyes and had a light sleep. I was on guard for anything that could happen today.

When Peter woke up, the sun was out. He motioned for us to be quiet and not wake Casey. She was so tired and stressed. I went with Peter, he let us out and cleaned up the mess. He was just finishing, when Casey came out to greet us.

She looked refreshed, good, she needed to be. Life was getting messy.

Casey's cell phone rang, she took it out of her pocket and answered it. Putting it down she got a smile on her face and walked over to Peter.

"Good morning Honey, guess what?" Casey asked.

"Good morning Casey, I wouldn't know what to guess." He placed the last of the mess in the garbage and turned to face her, waiting for the news.

I was waiting too.....

"That was Scott, his dad bought a house with him and it's in Boscastle! Only a hop, skip, and jump from here. They have decided to be here in the summer and return to Switzerland for the winter races. They plan on stopping by today before they head back home to Switzerland to put affairs in order and then come back here. Should we tell them of our mess?" Casey asked Peter.

"Well, they were really helpful with the last one, but both of them almost lost their lives. We can tell them about it and see if they want to help or if they can help us. Now, I need to wash up and let's get everyone fed." Peter led the way and we followed him into the house.

Casey was talking to him. "Great idea! You wash up, I'll feed the dogs and get some eggs and ham on the stove."

"Thank you Dear." Peter disappeared into the bathroom, I could hear the shower going. Casey was singing to us making us feel good as we ate our morning meal. We had been stressed too, she knew that.

Peter wasn't long, Casey had a hot meal on the table for them. Captain was just finishing his food, I was done and waited for scraps, so was T.J., Captain would catch-on when he got older how to eat fast and wait for something from the table.

"We need to stick around because the guys are stopping by. So, should we call the leader of the team that prosecutes Nazi's after breakfast and see what he can find for us about my grandfather?" Casey asked after she swallowed her last bite.

"Great idea! I'll clean up and you can get

your laptop, bring it in here so we can talk together on speaker phone." Peter said getting up and stacking the dishes in the sink.

"I'm so excited, I'm holding my breath!" Casey jumped up and ran into the other room, returning quickly with her laptop.

"Here's his website and number." Casey pulled out her phone. "They are just an hour ahead of us, so it's 10 A.M. there, here goes." The phone rang and someone answered.

"Hello, my name is Casey Lane, I found your website and I need your help if you can give it to me.

"Yes, I speak English, my name is Mr. Schim, what can I do for you Ms. Lane?"

"My husband and I just found out that my grandfather was in the MI-5 at the age of 27, right before WWll. I can't find any facts on him except that he lived in Buenos Aires before the war, he was in Argentina after the war for a bit, then he was in Africa, Iraq, Turkey and a few more places. His first wife was killed in the war, his second wife and son, my father, never knew he was in the MI-5. He told them he worked for the railroad. Then since we have been trying to find something out, people have been trying to kill us. We have been robbed, others have been murdered and hurt." Casey stopped because Mr. Schim interrupted her.

"Let me interrupt right there, if your lives are in danger then you are on to something. I need some more information, then I'll put that into my data base and have a full report for you this afternoon or tomorrow. I want you to use extreme caution from now on. After you get your story, only you can decide what to do with it, but we can come in and arrest any war criminals. It sounds like someone is covering for one. Here is my personal phone number and email." He gave it to Casey and she wrote it down. "Please give me your phone number, address and I will be in touch as soon as possible. Have a low profile until we find out what is happening Ms. Lane. Also, let me know if you plan on leaving the country to chase after any of these people, they are very dangerous."

"Yes, thank you Mr. Schim, my maiden name is Lane my married name is Anderson-

Lane. We will wait for your report." Casey gave him our address and her phone number, and then Casey hung up.

"Casey, it's a good thing you contacted him." Peter said wiping up the counter. Then he walked over and joined Casey at the table. "He has an impressive web site too. Let's put this aside and do some projects around here while we wait for Scott and Baron to arrive." Peter looked up, "I think I hear them now."

I barked and took off for the front door, T.J. was on my hills.

Peter opened the door to a smiling Baron and Scott!

"Welcome, come in, so happy to see you." Peter stood aside and let them enter.

"Thank you, it looks like you've settled in. What a pretty place." Baron said.

"Hi you guys!" Casey came out of the kitchen and hugged Baron. "Welcome to our little home."

"It's good to see you Dear." Baron laughed.

"Hi Scott!" Casey let go of Baron and hugged Scott.

"Hi Casey, wow, I guess we'll have to come visit more often. We only live 20 minutes from you!"

"Do you have pictures of your place?" Casey led Scott to the couch and Baron followed. Casey sat in between them. Peter pulled up a chair.

Baron pulled out photos. "Here are a few." He chuckled.

Casey looked at them. "It's adorable! A little white cottage on the cliff overlooking the beach."

"Yes, there is a garden shed, look here it is." He handed Casey another photo, while Peter looked through some too.

It was a wood garden shed, with windows and covered with a vine. It looked nice. I bet Peter could build one for Casey and us here too.

"Look Peter, is this what you were thinking of having done?" Casey handed Peter the photo.

"Yes, it is, I found one that's a garden cottage greenhouse that comes in pieces and you just have to put it together." Peter said.

"In this climate, you are going to need one, so I suggest you do it this summer." Baron said handing Peter some more photos.

"How's Carson City Spirit doing?" Casey asked.

"She is fine, I have her being watched and worked in our barn back home. We are going to try for the White Turf Races again this next year. It can't go wrong two years in row!" Baron laughed.

"Don't laugh, let us tell you what is happening here." Then Casey started in on her story of her grandfather, the lies, deception and the people after them, of Robert and Jack as well.

"Casey! We planned on going back to Switzerland to get some things, but we can send for things and have them sent to us. I hope you expect us to be a part of this with you? You are like a daughter to me and I don't want anything happening to you or Peter!" Baron paused.

"Oh Baron!" Casey leaned over and hugged him.

"I feel the same way about you and Peter,

Casey. You are like the brother and sister I never had." Scott looked at Casey and Peter with tears in his eyes. "We have been through so much together recently, I can't imagine a world without the two of you in it and all of the dogs."

"We feel the same way too Scott." Casey hugged him.

I walked over and gave Scott a high five.

T.J. wagged his tail.

Peter got up, "I need to call the hospital and see how Jack is doing, he wasn't doing well last night." Peter excused himself.

"Casey, I didn't realize that your friend, Jack may not make it?" Baron said.

"He wasn't doing well last night, they weren't sure he would make it. Robert, his brother, was doing better when we left them." Casey barely finished and Peter came into the room. His face looked grim.

Casey jumped up. "Honey, how are the boys? How's Jack?"

"Casey, Jack had a transfusion, he's in critical condition. Robert can be released, I told them I'd come down and help Robert. I'm sorry

Baron and Scott, do you mind?" Peter asked.

"My dear son," Baron said, "we will go with you. Get your things together Casey."

"Ok, boys, you're in charge of the house. Don't let anyone in! We'll be back shortly." Casey rubbed my head and then did the same to T.J. and Captain.

I wagged my tail and laid down by the couch.

"Peter, all of you go out, I'll put on the alarm so that the dogs will be safe." Casey grabbed her coat and gave us a second glance before she walked out the door after the others. Everyone was talking at once. Then silence. Casey didn't even leave on any music for us. I sighed. Oh well. I shut my eyes and fell asleep.

I woke up and looked out. It was getting dark! Casey, Peter, Baron and Scott left around one pm, that was hours ago! Where were they? I looked out the window and saw the sun setting. I looked back at T.J., he was aware of the night approaching as well.

Where were they?????

12

THEN AS IT got darker and darker, I paced and paced. There was a knock on the window that I had been watching. I ran over to it and saw Scott!

"Jackie Lee, go over to the door boy and unlock it." I think that's what he said. I ran over to the door and looked at the lock. Actually, I thought I could unlock it.

I stood up and put my front paws on the door, then took my right paw and grabbed the latch. It took me a few times but I finally got it and Scott opened the door. Then the alarm went off.

Scott reached over and put in a code. "Casey gave it to me as I got away guys! The hospital is in lock down, there was an attack from who knows who. Casey slipped mc the code and told me to get home to you guys."

Scott locked the door back up and turned on the TV. The news came on and we could see the live standoff on TV. Terrorists were in the hospital holding hostages. The worst fears gripped me, I couldn't think for a minute, then it hit me! We had to go save them! I looked at T.J., he was thinking like me.

I barked at Scott. He was glued to the TV. He looked over at me. "Oh, let me feed you guys. Lead the way Jackie Lee."

What the heck, we need nutrition if we were going to save everyone.

I led Scott into the kitchen and showed him where our food was.

He pulled out the food and then took some paper plates and dumped food out for all of us.

He made a sandwich for himself too. Then he surprised me!

"Boys, we're going in free them!"

13

I BARKED AND so did T.J., then after scarfing my food I jumped up by the kitchen door and grabbed three leashes and dropped them at Scott's feet. He laughed and picked them up.

"Ok, ok, I know you're in a hurry Jackie Lee, let Captain finish. We need a plan too. Hmmm. When we get there let me go and talk to the police, perhaps they will have a plan for us." Scott snapped my leash on and T.J.'s too, then he went over and hooked up Captain, who was just taking his last bite.

Scott loaded us into the back seat of his Mercedes and off we went. It wasn't long before we arrived on the scene, what a scene it was! Scott parked and got out walking over to one of the local cops. He looked over at the car and saw me, then smiled at Scott.

"Let me guess, Jackie Lee wants to help?" he said, as he walked over and let me out of the car. I recognized him, it was Officer Harrison!

"Yes, that's about the size of it." Scott looked into the car nervously. "I was in there," he pointed at the hospital, "and got out before they rounded everyone up in the cafeteria on the first floor. There are only three of them, they were shouting things in German and waving guns around. They were looking for something or someone." Scott stopped because the look on the cop's face stunned him. "Um, what part of that did you want to know more about?" he asked.

"Well, first of all, who are you and why are you with Jackie Lee?" The cop asked.

"I'm Scott, a dear friend of Casey and Peter's, my dad and I came down for a visit and then we drove them to the hospital to visit Jack." Scott answered.

Officer Harrison answered, "They have killed one person inside already, they are Nationalists or Nazi's, they have to be after something Jack knows, or maybe Casey has. Is there anyway Jackie Lee can go with us around to the back? We have decided to storm into the place from the front, while having a team in the back to sneak in and free the rest of the hostages. I don't know what is happening to the people in the hospital rooms that need attention? This needs to end. Wait here, I'll be right back." Officer Harrison stalked off hurriedly.

I looked at T.J. and Captain.

Are you guys up to saving them? I'm going!

T.J. barked yes and to my surprise, so did Captain.

Officer Harrison came back with two other young police officers. They didn't have any visible body armor, I was shocked they had guns, they looked too young.

We followed them around to the back of the hospital. Officer Harrison opened a door, whew! No alarm went off! He motioned for T.J. and me to go ahead of him. Captain stayed in the back with Scott.

I walked down the hallway, trying to not tap my nails on the concrete and make any noise. I stopped, I heard shouting, the cafeteria was just around the corner. I snuck up and peaked, there was Casey!!! I told T.J. and we had a plan. Officer Harrison was behind us.

"Boys, can you attack those gunmen?" He pointed at the one holding a gun and watching the hostages, the other was walking around shouting out questions.

I gave him a high five. He counted silently to five, then we went. I flew into the room biting the arm of the gunman pointing it at Casey and the others. T.J. knocked over the gunman walking around, Peter knocked the gun out of his hand and one young officer put cuffs on him. Baron jumped up grabbed the gun out of the gunman I had pinned. That left one more, he came back into the room and before he knew what was happening I had jumped on his stomach and bit his arm, Scott and one of the nurses grabbed his other arm and kicked the gun out of his hands. They looked like skin heads, shaved heads, tattoos on their arms and earrings in their ears. Young punks didn't look too hot now!

Casey ran over and hugged me. "Thank

you, Jackie Lee, what a good boy."

Peter had T.J. in his arms, and Captain too.

"Scott, thank you for coming in and saving us, they killed one doctor!" Casey was chocked up.

"Are you kidding, we couldn't do nothing! Our family was in here, we're a team Casey." He hugged her.

"Great job Son," Baron came over and hugged his son.

"Thanks dad, but it was Jackie Lee and T.J. that did the work." Scott ruffled my ears. I wagged my tail.

The cops came in and took statements, nurses ran into the patient's rooms and checked on them.

We followed the nurse into Jack's room. He was still unconscious. Did the gunmen even know Jack was here? We were going to find out after the attackers were interrogated.

The closet door opened, we all turned and were ready to attack, when Robert shouted out, "Don't shoot, it's me! I was keeping my brother safe!"

Casey let out a laugh as a sign of relief.

"I'm so glad you're alright!" Casey ran over and hugged him. "Are you feeling better?"
Robert chocked as he said, "I've been better, I have a head ache and I'm bruised, but I'm better off than my brother."

"You are at that young man," the doctor that entered the room said. He walked over to check Jack. "He is at least starting to breathe on his own. His ribs are cracked and what had us going was that he had an internal rupture, we operated on him before all of this happened. There will be police outside of the hospital and this room until his release. Robert, you had better either stay here, we'll get you a bed, or go home with your friends. Going back to your place is not safe; Officer Harrison told me to convey the message to you. I'm Doctor Vietti," he said as he looked up and shook Robert's hand.

"Well, I would like to stay here then," Robert answered.

Casey looked at Peter, he shook his head. "Robert, come home with us, we have an extra bedroom."

Robert looked up with tears in his eyes, "Will Jack be ok if I leave?" he asked Doctor Vietti.

"Yes, he will, it would be best you go get a hot shower, warm meal and good night sleep. Tomorrow will be another day and you will look better if you're rested."

Robert looked over at Casey. "If I won't be in the way I would appreciate it."

"The more the merrier, Baron and Scott are staying with us too tonight. We can set cots up in the living room and the extra bedroom. I feel it's better we all stick together for now." Peter came over and put his arm around Casey.

"I feel the same way." Peter said looking at Robert, then Baron and Scott. "We are family, and we have a lot more to do to solve this case. Let's say we go home?"

"I'm all for that." Casey said grabbing her hand bag.

"So am I, let me go pick up a pizza for us on the way back. OH, wait, we have just our car?" Baron looked at Scott.

"Yes, how about I drive Casey, Peter and the dogs home, then come back here and get you and Robert?" Scott suggested.

Baron looked at Peter and Casey, "Is that ok with you two?"

"Great idea, is it ok with you Robert?" Peter asked looking at Robert.

"Yes, I'll be able to sit with my brother for a bit." Robert went over and sat in a chair by his brother.

"Ok, it's settled, let's go." Scott led the way and we followed him out.

I couldn't wait to get home and knew Casey couldn't either, there had better be no more surprises tonight!

"Casey, or Peter, what was that all about back there? Do you have any idea at all?" Scott asked.

"I gathered they were wanting drugs out of the hospital, the doctor that got shot swallowed the key to drug cabinet and one of the guys went ballistic. Then all chaos broke out! The next thing we knew, everyone in the hospital was a hostage. They were some sort of terrorist group and perhaps one of their members needed the medicine. At least that's what I got out of it. How about you Casey?" Peter looked at Casey and put his arm around her.

"That's what I got out of it too, except I can't think that it was some kind of diversion for something else. At first, I thought they were there to kill Jack and Robert. I'm glad Robert is coming to stay with us, I wish Jack would heal and we could get him out too." Casey sighed. "I'm exhausted and I know all of you are too, I'll just be glad to get home, eat, bathe and sleep. All in that order."

"I hear you, honey. Scott, you and your dad are very dear to us, that you for being here for us tonight." Then Peter added, "Again."

I knew he was referring to the St. Moritz case, that's where we met Scott and his dad, Baron. What more could happen? I guess I was too tired to think about it. We were home before I knew it. We got out of the car and Scott left to pick up the pizza Baron had ordered, and then Baron and Robert still waiting at the hospital.

Peter disengaged the alarm and went in

first to check out the house, making sure we were safe.

"All clear," Peter shouted from the kitchen.

Casey let T.J., Captain and me into the house before her, then she shut the front door. I went over and looked out of the window, I didn't see anything so followed Casey into the kitchen. Peter had the table set and the wine opened. He poured Casey a glass.

"Cheers, sweetheart to surviving our first month of marriage." Peter clanked his glass against Casey's.

"Yes, cheers, here's to solving this case and going on vacation!" Casey laughed.

I looked at the wall behind the table, something was there we hadn't noticed. I walked around the table and sniffed, then scratched.

"Jackie Lee," Casey called, getting up from the table, "What is it boy?" She walked over to where I was scratching and then Peter came over too.

"It's a door, Casey." Peter looked at her, "It's flush with wall, there's no handle." He said looking around the wall.

There was a picture of Cornwall on the wall next to the outline of the door. Casey took it off the wall and behind it was a switch.

"Stand back Peter and Jackie Lee." Casey moved the lever and the door opened swinging out into the kitchen.

It was pitch black and hard to see inside, Peter stuck his hand in and felt along the wall. The light went on. All of us looked inside, there were stairs going down under the house.

"Good grief Casey! I bet there is something down there that the thieves want. I hear the others coming home now, let's show them." Peter left us and went to let the others in.

Scott, Baron and Robert carried pizza's that they placed on the table.

"Look what Jackie Lee found!" Casey pointed at the staircase.

"You just discovered this?" Baron asked.

"Yes," Casey answered.

"Let's eat and then go down, this just gets more and more exciting! Baron replied.

Casey handed out hand wipes and put paper plates down. Peter poured the wine and everyone sat down contemplating the evening and what we would find after dinner.

I was so excited I couldn't wait for them to eat and go down the stairs. I walked over and peered down to have a look, there was a handrail on the left, a wall on the right.

"Jackie Lee, wait a minute for us boy." Peter got up and took a flashlight from the top of the refrigerator.

"Ok, whose game? I know Jackie Lee and T.J. are ready." Peter laughed.

Casey jumped up, "You're not leaving me out."

"I'm game too!" Baron and Scott said at the same time, looking at Robert.

"I'll clean up, call me if something neat happens, call me if you need help too. I believe someone should stay up here." Robert grabbed the plates and started cleaning up the food.

"That's a good idea." Peter told him, "If we find anything interesting you will know."

"Ok, thanks." Robert said.

I took off down the stairs in front of everyone, T.J. was right behind mc. I reached the bottom of the stairs and it was dark, so I waited for Peter to bring the flashlight.

Peter moved the flashlight all around and saw a switch on the wall next to him. He turned it on and the room flooded with light. All of us looked around the room. It was incredible! The room was decorated in antiques and collectibles, Casey passed me and started uncovering objects. All we could do was gasp when she took the first cover off the object!

14

CASEY HAD UNCOVERED a beautiful carousel horse!

"What was Grandpa doing with this?" Casey was amazed.

"I don't know, but look!" Peter uncovered another one. It was different in color and bigger than this one.

"Wow!" Baron was amazed as well. "Scott, can you go get Robert? He would love to see this."

"Sure dad, this is amazing, it looks like there are more things in here as well. They are so well preserved!" Scott took off up the stairs to get Robert.

Peter, Casey and Baron uncovered three in all. Some were in better condition than others, two of them were heavy, really heavy, like something might be in them! Boy, we had hit a gold mine with this house! I hoped Casey felt the same way.

Robert came down the stairs and a huge grin spread across his face. "These are amazing! Are there any names on them?"

Robert walked over and looked at one fabulous carousel horse, then at the base of it and the words Michael Dentzel was stamped on it.

"We need to look up the maker, they are gorgeous, of course these are only three of the many horses on a carousel, after we finish up with Grandpa's first mystery, we need to dig into this one. I hope I can wait; it will give us time though to do some research." Casey sounded like she was asking for approval for waiting.

Ha, ha, I knew her so well, she would be digging into this before anyone of us realized what was happening.

"I suggest we cover these back up and go back upstairs, securing this room. I feel there are some treasures down here, but I agree Casey, we need to fix this other mess so we stop getting chased and some of us hurt." Baron started helping Peter cover the pretty horses up.

Sitting around the fireplace, sipping tea everyone had a lot to talk about.

"This house has so many hidden secrets, my grandfather was a character." Casey laughed.

"His granddaughter is a chip off the old block, my dear." Baron chuckled.

"I am so sure now that my parent's death was not an accident. I would love to find out what they were doing and why they had to be taken out." Casey said woefully. "I never got to know them, they were killed when I was young and why did I never get to meet my dad's parents? It isn't fair, life isn't fair. What did my grandfather have to hide? What was he after? Do you think we will ever find out?"

"Honey, I don't know, but we will do everything we can to find out. We need to know why Jack is in the hospital, why people are snooping around here, why you were almost run down. There are just too many things happening that we need to find answers for." Peter put his arm around her and kissed her cheek.

Everyone agreed that we had to find some answers. Baron and Scott were in it for the long run, they assured us.

"I'm sorry my brother and I took the assignment from these thugs. We wouldn't be in this situation if we hadn't, but we wouldn't have met all of you either. Tomorrow I need to go sit with Jack, hopefully he will recover soon. They have the room guarded, I don't think this situation tonight was about us. They didn't search rooms, they were just demanding drugs from the nurses. Can we call the hospital and see how my brother is doing before we call it a night?" Robert asked Casey.

"Yes, here's my cell phone or I can call for you, Robert. Whatever suits you. I'm so glad you and Jack came into our lives. It's funny how we met though, isn't it?" Casey laughed.

"It is, I'm sorry, Casey and Peter." Robert chuckled.

"Can you call for me Casey?" Robert asked.

"Yes." Casey stood up and walked over to the window.

"Thank you." Robert replied.

"No problem." Casey answered. Just then the hospital must have picked up, because she was talking to someone.

Casey hung up, "He is resting and they took him off the ventilator, he's breathing on his own!!! That's great news. Also, the incident tonight had nothing to do with either of you, but they are keeping a guard outside of his room and extra patrols around the hospital."

"Thank you, Casey, that's great news!" Robert jumped up and hugged Casey.

"No problem." Casey laughed.

Then everyone settled down to talk about our plans.

Peter grabbed his IPad and started searching Michael Dentzel; to find out about the carousel horses he designed. Peter was reading off what he found. It was very exciting, but I fell asleep as Peter's voice drifted in and out of my dreams.

15

THE NEXT MORNING, I followed Casey downstairs, Baron was in the bedroom, Robert had taken the couch and Scott was asleep on the air mattress with Baron snoring away snugged in his arms. I looked at Casey and she smiled, putting her finger to her lips, "Shhhhh." Casey motioned me to the kitchen as T.J. came bounding down the stairs.

Casey took both of us out through the kitchen to relieve ourselves. It was snowing lightly and a bit chilly. We needed to get a load of wood for the coming months, unless we planned on going somewhere. Knowing us, we never made plans, we just did things that made sense. Casey called us back in and she made a pot of coffee, the smell of the coffee brought Baron into the kitchen.

"My Dear, good morning, I slept very well. After breakfast Scott and I will go out or you can come with us and I'll buy a load of groceries. By the looks of the weather we might be needing some firewood delivered too, do you have a local phone book I can look through? I'll order some wood too. Thank you." Baron took the cup of coffee Casey handed him and sat down.

"I don't want you to buy the food and wood, Baron!" Casey said sitting down across from him.

"It's the least I can do Dear; I want to do this. Then later on today, Scott and I need to go check on our house. I have a shipment of furniture and belongings being delivered this week." Baron said through sips of coffee.

"Oh, that reminds me!" Casey just remembered something. "Our bedroom furniture arrives today!!! Are you in need of some futons? We have the air mattress which is easier to store than the futons."

"Actually, we have a bedroom we could put the futon in, Casey. Perhaps they can deliver it to our house after dropping off your furniture." Baron was just finishing his coffee, when Peter walked in.

"Good morning everyone. Ohh, good coffee." Peter grabbed a cup and filled it up.

"Good morning Sweetheart." Casey said, "Could you bring the pot over and fill up Baron's cup?"

"Good morning Peter, thank you." Peter just filled up his cup. "I was just talking to Casey about ordering some wood for us here today and filling up the cabinets with food. Then the futon can be delivered to my house after your furniture arrives. We have a very busy day." Baron said thoughtfully looking through the phone book Casey had given him.

"Great plan, I was going to remind you Casey about the furniture today. Let me make some pancakes and bacon, then I can get Robert to the hospital." Peter couldn't finish because Baron interrupted.

"Great, I'll take Scott and we will load up with food; Casey can stay here and wait for the furniture, then I can follow the moving van to my place. While you make breakfast, I'm going to get everyone up and take a shower. If that's ok with you?" Baron stood up.

"It's great, but after breakfast why don't you take Casey shopping, I'll stay here, you guys can drop off Robert. Scott and I can be here when the furniture comes and we can follow the moving van; then get your house set up." Peter looked at Baron for approval.

"Ah, great plan, yes, yes, that will work better, indeed it will. I bet there's someone at the grocery store selling wood, I'll take care of that too." Baron was thinking, then he said, "Ok, make sure you guys pick up some clothes for me and whatever we will need here. I'm off to hit the shower." Baron got up from the table and walked into the other room, dropping hot coffee off for each of them.

"Yes, we will pick up your clothes and whatever the two of you need." Peter called off after him. Then he looked at Casey.

"How are you holding up, Casey?" Peter put his arm around her and she laid her head on his shoulder.

"Fine, when this is done, can we have a real honeymoon?" Casey asked.

"Yes, I've been thinking the same thing,

start thinking about where we should go or what you want to do. Let me start breakfast now Honey." Scott excused himself and got up to cook one of his outstanding breakfasts.

Scott gave us some pancakes and cooked hamburger, it was yummy. He made an extra plate for Captain too.

Breakfast was over and dishes were cleaned. Casey, Baron and Robert left the house; I used my sad look and got to go with them!

Baron drove to the hospital first and dropped off Robert, he said he would call when he was ready to come back home.

"Give Jack our love." Then Casey had a thought, "Why don't we just stop back by and see him too when we're done? I would love to see him and we can pick you up then." Casey looked at Robert with a grin.

Robert looked back at Casey as he was getting out of the car, "That works for me. I know my brother would love to see you. Casey, thank you for your kindness, you too Baron."

"It's ok kid," Baron said with an emotional voice.

"Robert, how could we not care? Both of you are part of our team and family now. Have a nice visit and we should be back in about two hours." Casey shouted out the window, as Robert waved goodbye.

We went to the local store; I had to sit outside and wait while Baron and Casey loaded up the carts with food for all of us. I sat there watching them as people came out and pet me; saying what a nice doggy I was. I just thumped my tail. I was watching Casey; I didn't have time to socialize. It seemed like forever before they came out of the store. I jumped up to greet them when they walked my way.

"Good boy Jackie Lee," Casey leaned over and kissed me. "Get back in the car Jackie Lee."

I jumped in and made room for the grocery bags, then Baron went back and brought out a cart full of wood for our fireplace. We were in Baron's vehicle so there was plenty of room, everything fit into the back end of the SUV and I sat in the back seat.

"The furniture should have arrived already Baron. I'm excited to see how everything looks in the house." Casey looked back at me, "Right Jackie Lee?"

You bet, a bigger bed, YES!!!! I gave her my paw letting her know I understood what she was saying to me.

We arrived at the hospital and I got to go inside. It was because I had my armor on and looked so official, but Casey said it was so I didn't eat all of the groceries, hehe.

Robert and Jack were talking as we walked in.

"Hi Jack, you look so much better! When are you able to get out of here?" Casey asked.

"Hi Casey, I feel a lot better too. They said maybe tomorrow, but Robert and I were talking, we can't go back to our house right now. We were trying to decide where to go." Jack looked worried.

"No worries!" Casey told him, "You can come stay with us. We have extra futons now, plus we have German Shepherd security! You will be welcomed and safe with us." Casey looked at Baron, "Can you call Scott and ask Peter not to load up the futons to take to your house?"

"I'm right on it, Casey." Baron had his phone to his ear.

"Robert told me you offered, but I hate to impose on you, really I do. We could go visit our cousins in London." Jack was looking like he didn't really want to go visit his cousins.

"No, I insist you stay with us. Otherwise how can you help us solve this case? We need both of you, if you're up to it." Casey pleaded.

"I want to stay and help," Robert looked at Jack, "If it becomes too much of a burden on you Casey, we can go to London. Deal Jack?"

"Ok, but I won't be able to do much for a while. Except, I'm really good on the computer and that is something I can do. I can research what you need." Jack was getting excited now. "I wonder if I could get out tonight? I can walk, just not for long. Can you get the nurse for me Casey or Baron?"

"I'll find your doctor," Baron turned to leave, "Have Robert get your things together. The sooner you're out of here, the safer you will be." Baron left.

"I'll help Robert, show me what to do

Jack." Casey offered.

By the time Baron found the doctor, we were all packed, so when he entered the room he had to agree that it was best for Jack to vacate his room. Jack was overjoyed, just a day ago he was nearly critical and improved so quickly. It must be because he was so youthful, is what Baron kept saying, that is how he recovered that fast.

We drove home, Scott and Peter were gone, T.J. and Captain had gone with them, hmm. So, it was just us. We got Jack inside and set him up in the guest room. There was a futon set up in there for Robert. After that Casey and I went upstairs, WOW! I raced for the bed and jumped on it,

He He!!! I was jumping and racing around it.

"Jackie Lee!!!!, you're messing up the bed! Stop!" Casey ran over and jumped on top of me. I looked at her from under her arms and she started laughing hysterically. She rolled off me and I bounced back onto her.

Baron came bounding up the stairs to see what the commotion was all about and he started laughing at the site.

"Ok, you two, let's remake your bed Casey, before Peter comes back." Baron came over and grabbed me, laughing as he did it, then picked me up and sat me down. "Stay Jackie Lee." Then he grabbed Casey's hands and pulled her up and off the bed.

"Thank you for rescuing me Baron. Look at this mess!" Casey was still chuckling as Baron helped her remake the bed.

It was some kind of great bed!

There was a noise downstairs; Peter, Scott, T.J. and Captain were home!!! I raced down the stairs to greet everyone. Casey and Baron followed me.

"Wow, you brought a lot of stuff over, thanks guys. Scott can you help me unload the wood and groceries?" Baron asked.

"Sure Dad, let me set this down"

"I can help too!! Casey chimed in.

"We can get it Casey," Baron told her, "You have things to do, I'm sure." Then Baron and Scott excited the house.

Robert came out, "I'll help them, Casey,

you've done enough for today." Robert ran out to grab the bags of groceries.

Peter and Casey unloaded the groceries in the kitchen. "Jack got released, so he's in the guest room, Honey." Casey told Peter, as she grabbed some chips and poured them into a bowl, then put some dip in another bowl. Peter handed her paper plates and napkins. Together they picked up everything to take into the living room.

"That's great news, Casey! I'll put this down and go in and see him." Peter helped Casey arrange the table in the living room and put the snacks out. Then we went to see Jack.

Casey went back into the kitchen and made some drinks for everyone; Baron walked into the kitchen and helped her carry everything out. Scott came in from outside with Robert, carrying some wood. Robert went over and got the fireplace going.

"There's some snacks and drinks out before dinner." Casey said, "We are having steaks tonight, Peter is grilling them, with some sweet potatoes and salad. This is just to keep everyone from being too hungry."

"Thank you, Casey," Robert said, "Let me clean up and I'll be right out."

Peter came out with Jack and sat him in the comfy chair by the fireplace. Then Scott took out a TV tray and put some chips and dip on it for Jack.

"What do you want to drink, Jack?" Scott asked him.

"With my meds, probably some tea, if it's not too much trouble, thank you." Jack replied.

"No problem," Scott went into the kitchen and made some tea for anyone that wanted some.

In the meantime........

T.J. have you checked out that bed?

Yeah, Jackie Lee, but Peter wouldn't let us on it!

He he, I just had a heyday jumping in it. Casey and Baron remade it. What about Captain, should we get him to go jump on it?

Jackie Lee! Only if I get to do it too!

Ok, T.J. let's go get Captain and we can all see how we fit on it!

T.J. and I took off for the kitchen where we

found Captain getting snacks from Peter while he fixed dinner.

"There you two are, come on, I have some snacks for you and then I have your dinner made." Peter threw us some raw meat bits.

I think we should skip the bed jumping right now. I said with my mouth full.

If you want to stay on Peter's good side, I say you are correct in your thinking, Jackie Lee.

Captain heard us, but chose to ignore the conversation. He never did anything wrong and never got into trouble. He was probably the perfect German Shepherd.

Peter fed us and then we joined the adults in the living room as they ate. I was really hoping for something to fall off a plate, but it didn't, then dinner was interrupted.

Casey answered her cell phone and her face went pale. "Yes, I understand, yes." Casey dropped her phone.

"Casey," Peter jumped up to go to her.

Casey looked around at everyone. "Aunt Claire has been kidnapped!"

16

"CASEY!" SCOTT JUMPED up and looked at his dad.

I bet he was thinking, what can happen next. I looked at T.J. and we both ran over to Casey.

"Honey, what did they say? Who was it?" Peter was desperate to find out what had just transpired.

"It was the police, Aunt Claire's neighbor noticed she hadn't seen her for a day and became worried. She went over to Aunt Claire's and found the door unlocked, so she went in expecting the worst. Instead she saw the place a mess and a note was stuck on her rocking chair. She called the police and they went through the place looking for fingerprints and clues. We have to go to the police station here tomorrow at 10 a. m., the officer that first went into her house will be there to meet us. Hopefully we can come to some conclusion or find some clues." Casey looked at Peter, "I need a glass of wine, please. I'm so upset! I'm glad I was full or I couldn't have finished my dinner."

Peter came over with a glass of savory Bordeaux and placed it in front of Casey. "It just keeps getting weirder and weirder. This has to be the craziest case we have been on."

"Amen to that." Baron was shaking his head. "Let me clean up, Casey, you and Peter go sit by the fire and relax. Come on Scott and Robert, let's clean up. Jack, you can go sit in your chair by the fire, we won't be long."

"Thank you, Baron," Casey got up and Peter took her wine, following her over to the couch. "Just sit down here and relax Honey." Then Peter sat down next to her and they talked.

Jack didn't go sit down, he went into the kitchen with his brother, Baron, and Scott.

"Casey, let's meet the officer in the morning. Then perhaps we should look at taking a break, we still haven't had our honeymoon. Perhaps we should get away while they are looking for your Aunt Claire, will you think about it? Please?" Peter reached over caressingly kissing her lips.

Casey put her arms around Peter and let out a sigh. "Yes, we need a break Honey. You know something funny? Sophia, Kanani, Gunther the dragon and the rest of the crew are living in this area in another time! Wrap your head around that one! LOL. Maybe we should go back and visit them. That would take us far away from these people that are after us." Casey laughed. "What?"

"That is something to wrap your head around, Casey. Imagine, time traveling! To think you and Jackie Lee did just that! Maybe someday, but we need to solve this situation before it gets anymore out of hand. Your aunt had better be ok; they don't know what they are up against. We are going to find these people and put them in prison!" Peter looked happy all of a sudden.

Casey unwrapped her arms around Peter and looked at him. "You're right! These people don't know how capable we are of catching crooks! Ha, my aunt will be fine, we have something they want or have access to get. If they don't get it, they won't harm her. I can't wait until morning." Casey took a sip of her wine and leaned over to scratch my ears.

I thumped my tail. I love you Casey.

Baron came into the room. "Everything is cleaned up Casey and Peter. Do you mind if I join you?"

Casey patted the couch, "Come sit right here."

Baron walked over and sat next to Casey, turning to both of them he gave them some encouragement. Casey and Peter knew that they had a lifetime friend in Baron.

Scott and Robert helped Jack get ready for bed. The two young men had the bedroom downstairs, Robert stuck out his head and said goodnight from both of them. Scott came out to the living room and picked up a book. He sat in the easy chair by the fire. Both Baron and Scott were sleeping in the living room tonight. It was quite cozy, having such a huge household in this little place. It was nice to feel like we had so much family. Casey and I had always been alone before. Sophia and Kanani had so many people in their lives too, it was fun visiting them. I dozed off and dreamed of Gunther, the dragon. I dreamed I ran into him again in Cornwall, or someplace around here. I must have been running in my sleep because Casey woke me up.

"Come on boy, it's outside then bed." Casey scratched my ears.

I groggily looked around, I noticed T.J. was already upstairs, Captain was snuggled in bed with Scott. I got up and followed Casey outside. I made it quick, it was cold out, then I ran in and beat her up the stairs. Scott and T.J. were already asleep. So, I snuggled next to Casey. Tomorrow would bring better things. I was sure of it.

It was a restless night and I know Casey didn't get a good night's sleep. I can sleep through anything, but I kept an eye on her. After all, Casey was mine and I was hers, I couldn't remember my doggie mom, just Casey.

Night zzzzzzzz.

There was a big noise outside! Peter jumped out of bed, Casey grabbed her phone, "Peter it's 2 a.m., what's the racket?"

Peter was looking out the window that was on the west side of the house; it overlooked the ocean. "Casey, it appears someone is firing off big rocket fireworks at us!"

17

"PETER, CASEY! GET DOWN here I'm calling the police and fire department!"

That was Baron, so I shot out of bed and raced T.J. down the stairs. Peter was right behind me. "Good Baron, thank you!" Peter glanced in on Robert and Jack. "Get out of the house guys!

"Casey, come on, make sure Captain comes too, hurry!!!" Peter raced out the front door after he grabbed his coat. Scott and I followed him.

Peter ran to the side of the house; Scott was right behind him. Peter ran over to the hose, grabbed it turned it on and started spraying the house. Then he shouted for Scott to do the same in the back of the house. Scott took off running. Casey ran out and helped Peter. Baron ran out into the street to have the neighbors make room for the fire truck and police. Robert helped Jack get out safely, after wrapping a blanket around him. T.J. and Captain came up to me.

Unbelievable Jackie Lee! It's one thing after another! Maybe we should go back to Sandy Island?

No, T.J., remember what happened there? We'll get through this. Maybe even have some fun while we get these guys.

Captain, back up, the fire truck is here! T.J. nudged him out of the driveway.

Woof! Captain barked and wagged his tail, then moved out of the way.

There was so much commotion I didn't know where to start. I ran around checking on everyone. The fireman put the fire out on the side of the cliff. The police had a car down on the beach, they knocked out the launch pad and seized the rest of the rockets. Another squad car arrived on the beach and they got out to look for the suspects. All of the neighbors were out; someone brought over coffee for the adults. Our house was ok, but the grass was singed right up to the garden. Luckily, Scott had doused the garden and it didn't burn. After what seemed like an eternity, the police came up to talk to

Peter, Casey and Baron. They took statements, photographs, and talked to neighbors to see if anyone knew anything. By the time they left it was early dawn and you could see the damage done to the property. There was a bombed out-car, still burning on the beach. It looked eerie and felt eerier. Neighbors started showing up with tons of food for all of us, that was nice, I was so hungry. Casey and Peter ate, then got ready to go to the police station. I wanted to go with them, but Casey made T.J. and me stay home to protect the house and everyone in it. Baron decided to clean house, so I laid in a corner and slept. When Casey and Peter came back, the house was so neat and clean. All of the sleeping bags, the guest bedroom, and kitchen were clean. Baron had loaded his vehicle with everything now ready for departure.

"Baron, what is going on?" Casey questioned Baron, she was perplexed and wanted to know as soon she walked in the door, Peter was right behind her.

"Scott and I have made a decision, we are going to our cottage, taking Robert and Jack with us. You and Peter should come too. I have four bedrooms, so no one is in the living room, like they are here. Now, if the two of you and the dogs want to come with us, please do. We have more space than you do, in fact I think it might be a better choice for you to come with us, thinking about it." Baron looked thoughtful.

"Well, let's sit down and talk, we have news as well." Casey pulled off her coat and sat on the couch. Peter sat next to her, Baron and the boys all sat down too.

"Here goes, Aunt Claire was kidnapped. The note said that the kidnappers wanted the map that was hidden in this house. They were taking her to South America and we could exchange Aunt Claire for the map there, in Brazil. I have the address here." Casey pulled it out.

"Casey? A Brazilian map?" Baron asked.

"There was a map, I took it out of the chest before we handed it over to you, Robert and Jack. Let me go get it." Casey got up and went upstairs, she came back down with a map in her hands. Casey carefully spread it out on the floor, everyone crowded around it. Peter helped Casey spread it out, the map was very large and somewhat fragile.

"Look here," Casey pointed to a dot on the map. "This is in Brazil, there were dots along this point, then X. Casey placed her finger over the X." Something of value must be buried here. There are too many horrid things happening for it to be nothing."

"I have to agree." Baron looked on. "I think you, Casey and Peter need to go down there. Scott and I can run things from up here with Robert and Jack."

"I second that." Scott quickly added.

"I'm just glad you didn't give us the map!" Robert looked a Casey, "Look what they did to Jack, they wouldn't think twice of killing us both if they had gotten that!"

"I'm in agreement, Robert and I goofed up big time getting involved and then you had to save our lives, Casey. Thank you." Jack was choked with emotion.

"I wouldn't say I saved your lives, because you got very hurt Jack, but you are going to be ok. Baron, could Captain stay with you if we go?"

"Absolutely! Scott and I wouldn't have it any other way my dear."

Peter looked at Casey, "It's settled then. T.J. and Jackie Lee will come with us to Brazil. Let's check some cruises to South America Casey. It would be more romantic to go by ship." Peter gave Casey a knowing glance.

"Peter! That's a wonderful idea!" Casey wrapped her arms around her husband.

"Well then, I suggest you and Peter look for that cruise, then come over for dinner and sleep at our place." Baron stood up. "Where's your laptop Casey? Let's look at suitable cruises."

Casey pointed to the desk, "It's in that drawer Baron."

Baron retrieved the laptop and sat down next to Casey and Peter.

Casey logged in and started a search. "Here's one, Princess Cruises, leaves London (Southampton), England, no that doesn't go to South America. Hmmm, looks like we might have to fly to Fort Lauderdale, Florida and take a cruise from there. The Silver Muse has a trip in Oct, it's $10,575 a person." Casey frowned at Peter, "That's expensive!"

"Honey, we will just need to keep searching. It's going to be a trip of a lifetime and who knows what will happen in South America?" Peter grinned, then helped Casey look for more options.

"This is hilarious Peter! I'm texting an agent!" Casey was cracking up. "They are a bit surprised by the GSD's coming." LOL. "His name is Eamon. He said that Cunard or the Queen Mary 2 would be the correct ships. Let's have a look at both of them."

I leaned over Casey and had a look. Both ships looked really big. I liked the Queen Mary, I hoped they picked that one.

"Casey, let's book this one." Peter pointed to the Queen Mary. "She leaves in a week." Perfect timing and she leaves out of Southampton, but makes a stop to pick up passengers in Cornwall!!!! How convenient." Peter looked at Casey. "We had better get some lists together, we can't take too much on the ship but we will need some supplies."

"Oh, Peter, that looks great! Let me snap these tickets up before there aren't any left." Casey bought two tickets and two dog tickets.

Yippee!!! I started running around in circles and barking, then T.J. started. Captain hid behind Baron, poor dog.

"I think they know what they are going to get to do, Peter." Haha, Casey laughed.

Baron was laughing too; in fact, everyone was happy. Robert and Jack went into the bedroom and cleaned up after themselves, packing what they had. Scott cleaned up the living room, with Baron helping and taking loads of stuff out to his car. I followed Casey and Peter upstairs to pack some overnight things, then I helped Peter get our dishes, food and leashes. By the time we shut the door behind us no one would ever have known that 6 people and 3 dogs had just left. Neither did we notice anyone around that could be watching us. I checked twice to make sure. We arrived at Baron and Scott's cottage, it was nice, they had a dock on the water and a beautiful view of Boscastle.

The next week flew by with nothing drastic happening to us. It was a relief and I could see that Casey looked happier. The day arrived, Baron drove us to the docks and we were there 2 hours before the Queen Mary departed.

"Casey, you and Peter keep in touch with me." Baron kissed Casey on the forehead and shook Peter's hand.

"We will, Baron, this is exciting, who knows what will we will find and hopefully we will be coming home with Aunt Claire." Casey grabbed her purse and looked inside. "Whew, I have the map."

"Honey, I know; you need to stop worrying." Peter hugged her.

"Baron, thank you for watching Captain, we will keep in touch." Peter said.

"Great, Scott and I will keep looking in on your place too. Have fun!" Then Baron hugged Casey and shook Peter's hand and walked away.

"Bye!!!!" Casey and Peter called after him.

Ruff!!! I barked.

Ruff ruff! T.J. barked too.

We were shown to our cabin. We were on the upper deck and had an excellent view of the water. Our cabin was by the elevator for dinner and all of the other events.

Can you see me on the deck?

"Jackie Lee get in here!" *Casey didn't want me jumping over the edge. Boy was this going to be fun!!!! OH NO!!!*

18

WE WALKED BACK into our cabin, everyone was so happy until.....

"Casey! There are messages on your phone." Peter was staring at the phone with trepidation. He knew something wasn't right.

"What?" Casey picked up her phone off the table, her face turned white and she looked at Peter. "Lock the cabin door and the balcony, close the curtains."

Peter said, "Honey the cabin door is locked, we haven't opened the deck, but I'll close the curtains and you sit right there on that chair, I will join you soon." Peter checked the front door, it wasn't locked, so he locked it and then he went up the stairs into the bedroom and made sure the deck doors were locked. He pulled down the screens, made a quick look around the room, then came back down and made sure the deck doors by Casey were locked also. By the time Peter sat down Casey had some color back in her face.

"Ok, what is this about?" Peter sighed.

"I'll read the messages, first one, GET off the Ship!!! Urgent, Nazi sympathizer, Erich Schoultz, the most dangerous of the Nazi followers is on that cruise looking for you!! From Mr. Schim.

Casey, you didn't' contact him!!!! I was horrified, we weren't supposed to leave without letting him know!

"The next message,... E.S. had his men kidnap your aunt, she is being held in South America. He did this to get you to give up looking for whatever your grandfather was after. He is on that cruise himself to oversee his men capture and torture you! You must be careful. Here is a photo of him, but he wears disguises. Also, we have put your friends in protective custody and your dog, Captain too. Please respond to this message as soon as you can. Mr. Schim~

"Casey, we are in grave danger, let's try to send him a text message back and ask what we should do."

"Ok Peter, boy have we screwed up getting on this ship. It's not going to be much of a honeymoon."

"I know Casey, but we will get out of this alive and find your Aunt Claire. She must be terrified!" Peter was upset but tried to be brave for us. "Honey, this was supposed to be a honeymoon, time to think on how we will get your aunt home safely, and solve the treasure mystery. We will be careful, we have a vague idea what this man looks like, but of course he will very likely be disguised and have others with him, hmm." Peter sighed and looked thoughtfully at Casey. He gave her a reassuring hug. Then he looked like he had an idea.

"I almost forgot!!! The biggest surprise yet!" Peter got up and ran over to a big box he had delivered onto the ship. I thought it was food and toys for T.J. and me but was I shocked!

"Peter, what are you talking about Honey?" Casey got up and followed him.

"Just wait," Peter opened the box carefully and pulled out another box, then handed it to Casey. "Be careful with this as you open it up,

Honey." Peter had a grin on his face.

"What on earth, Peter?" Casey was confused but very excited, her mind was taken off of their imminent danger.

Casey ripped open the box and there was a music case inside. She looked at Peter. Then took it out and placed it on the flat coffee table Peter had cleared off for her. Casey pulled out a beautiful violin!!!!!

"Peter!!!" Casey cried, "How did you know?"

"I remembered long, long ago when we were on Sandy Island and you were longing for this. I couldn't get yours but found the best one I could to replace it."

Casey opened the violin case and pulled out a Thomaz K. Kowalski violin!!!!

"Peter it's beautiful! Where did you find this?" Casey was amazed!

"I bought it online from Poland. This violin maker is amazing and I have heard many good things about his work. I thought it was a great investment, I have it fully insured too." Peter had outdone himself for sure!

"Well, it's been so long since I have played I will have to get lessons and practice. Thank you, Sweetheart, this is something that I will cherish always." Then Casey looked pensive, "Um, how will we keep it safe on this journey?"

"It can stay in our hotel room in South America with all of the things we brought along and with all of the dogs' things. No worries ok?" Peter came over and looked at the violin. "Can you play a few notes so we can hear the tone of it?"

"Yes," Casey smiled, she picked up the bow, chalked it and tuned the violin. "It was nothing to tune, wow." Casey put it up to her chin and played a tune. The tone of the violin was indeed gorgeous to listen to. It didn't even hurt T.J.'s ears or mine either.

"Casey that is a beautiful sounding instrument! I'm so happy it was a good decision on my part." Peter reached out and kissed her on the cheek.

Casey placed the violin in its case and turned around and put her arms around Peter. "Thank you from the bottom of my heart for such a wonderful gift as this, Peter." They engaged in a long kiss. Then Casey let go of Peter and turned around to clean off the violin, and put everything neatly back into its case.

"Where is a good spot for this Honey?"

"Casey, over here." Peter opened up the closet door. "This one has a lock on it, no one can get to it except us."

"Thank you, now we should see about

getting some food for all us." Looking at me, Casey said, "Do you and T.J. want to go for a walk and get some food?"

I barked, because of course I did!

Casey snapped a leash on T.J. and me too.

Then she put on the TV for noise, so it sounded like someone was in the cabin.

We walked out of the cabin, Peter went first to make sure that no one was outside waiting to get us. The coast was clear. To give a picture of the cabin we rented, here it is right from the Queen Mary 2 website.

We rode the elevator down a few floors and walked out onto the pool deck, there was so much activity, it looked like fun. I looked around to see if I saw anyone suspicious. Everyone just seemed to be enjoying themselves, so I followed Casey and Peter. They found a table out by the pool and sat down. There was a place for T.J. and me too. Peter ordered and food soon arrived!!! I was famished. We ate and then Casey and Peter took us down to the doggie kennels, there we went out on the dog grass and used the bathroom. Everyone was really nice down there. They asked if we wanted to stay with them, HA! That was the funniest thing I could think of. So, after Casey declined we left and went up a few decks to the shops. I was amazed nothing had happened to us yet, I guess I just expected something to happen after what we had been through.

We went back to our cabin and Casey checked reception for email. "I'm hooked up Peter, let me email Mr. Schim back, I can't text him from ship."

"Ok, Casey, tell him that it's too late for us

to get off, ask what he suggests except being careful." Peter sat down beside her.

"Ok, read this before I send it." Casey showed Peter the email.

"That's all we can do for now. Let's plan on an evening in our room, we have plenty of space and the deck to sit on as well, we just need to watch our surroundings."

Casey closed her laptop, "You're right, let's make some drinks and sit out on the deck. We need our energy for our rescue of Aunt Claire."

"I'm on top of that." Peter came back with two tall glasses full of ice and whatever he put in it. Casey unlocked the sliding doors and we walked out onto our private deck. We sat outside for a long time before Casey said they had to take us out again before bed. So sleepily I followed Casey and Peter took T.J. down to the pet area. They talked to other pet owners, there was one man that had a lot of questions but Casey excused us and found Peter.

"Honey, look at that guy over there, he's staring at me. I just got away from him, he was asking a lot of questions, something is strange about him, he has a strong accent too." Casey put her arm through Peters' arm.

Peter glanced over and the man turned away, he didn't have dog but was visiting the kennel, weird. "Maybe he just wants a dog." Peter joked.

Casey gave him a look.

"Alright I think he is weird too, maybe he's the spy that is going to get us." Peter whispered. I turned around and looked at him. The guy was watching us again! I nudged Casey to get going. That got her moving and when we got into the elevator and Peter hit the wrong floor. "We are going to the wrong floor and taking the stairs, I don't want this guy knowing which is our room."

"Smart thinking Peter." Casey gave him a kiss on the cheek. Peter looked at her and smiled.

We got out of the elevator and took the stairs down to our room. When the door opened and we stepped out, the man was there! HE HAD A GUN POINTED AT US!

19

"HOLD ON BUDDY, we have no fight with you. Put it down!" Peter commanded stepping in front of Casey to block her.

Casey pulled a canister of mace out of her pocket and slipped it stealthily into Peter's hand.

"You have been a sore spot with my men, too many times they have not been able to figure you out, all of you are coming with me." He pointed his gun and motioned for us to go ahead of him.

I was bewildered, I looked at T.J. and he looked at me. We had to do something! Then two men came running up to us from the other side of the hallway with their guns out. T.J. and I were thinking the same thing, I barked and both of us jumped the men. Peter attacked the first guy while I bit the guy I caught. Casey grabbed his gun before he got up and ran away. The guy T.J. got was screaming in agony, T.J. would not let go! Casey got his gun too and told him to stop the noise.

"Casey, I have this guy!" Peter yelled at the guy to stand up, Peter had the gun at his head.

"Peter, I have this guy too. Let's get them up to the Captain. There has to be some security on this ship that can contain them. T.J. good boy, let's go." T.J. let go and the guy awkwardly scrambled up the best he could.

T.J. was on the guy Casey was handling and I was on the guy Peter was shoving forward. It seemed to take forever, but we got to the bridge. Peter called for help and some crew members came out.

"Why do you have these men at gunpoint? Are you going to hurt us, rob us, hijack us?" The assistant crewmember nervously asked.

"No, these men attacked us at gunpoint. We caught two of them, there was one more, but he got away. They jumped us as we came out of the elevator on level 9. Is there anywhere to contain them?" Peter asked.

"Yes, just a minute." He left and went back inside, after a few minutes 3 men came out with cuffs. Without protests they cuffed the men. Peter and Casey handed over the guns.

"What will you do with them?" Casey asked.

"We have a place for criminals, we are too far out to sea or we would dock and hand them over to the local authorities. The Captain is on his way up to talk to you. Why don't you go into the office over there and wait?" Then he left with the two other men and took the ruthless men away. They looked back at us with an evil glare. There were still more out there and they knew it, so did we.

"Come on Casey, let's go into the office and wait, come on boys." We followed Peter.

"Peter, this is just the first night! How many more of them are there? What will happen next?" Casey was obviously shaken by this ordeal.

They continued to talk, the Captain finally came in and joined them.

"Good Evening, I'm Captain Jhona. This is bad business, please fill me in?"

"Nice to meet you, I'm Peter, this is Casey,

that's T.J. and Jackie Lee." Peter shook his hand.

"Nice to meet you and yes, we will fill you in." Casey shook his hand too.

"Ok, well where do you want to start? Please make yourselves comfortable."

Casey and Peter took turns and filled the Captain in, he didn't look too pleased but looked very interested.

"That is quite the story, too bad we are out in the middle of the ocean, there is no island or place to disembark." He reached for his phone and made a call, his face went pale. He dropped the phone and stood up. "We have been sabotaged!"

20

"ALL OF OUR COMMUNICATIONS are down. This is unheard of unless there is a bad storm. Why don't you have one of my officers take you to your room. I need to see if I can get to the bottom of this." Captain Jhona stood up to leave.

"Thank you, Captain, we would very much like an escort." Peter stood up and shook his hand. The Captain nodded and left.

After the Captain left, two officers came in to escort us. There was little talk until we got to our cabin.

"Let us go in and check out your room," One officer said.

"Ok, good idea." Peter grabbed Casey's hand.

Ten minutes later they came out.

"It seems ok, here is my card and a walkie talkie to call me if you need food or the dogs need to go out. My name is Officer Climmins, call for any reason, one of us will assist you. Keep your door locked. Good night, be careful."

"Thank you, Peter and Casey both said, as Peter took his card."

T.J. and I followed Peter and Casey into the room. I looked around, sniffing everywhere. I didn't smell anything out of sorts. So, I curled up next to the couch that Casey and Peter were sitting on. I dozed off as they talked. T.J. was snoring! As I looked up when Casey started up the stairs. "Bedtime kids." Casey called.

T.J. woke up, shook his head and looked around. I got up and got a drink and then followed him up the stairs.

It was a beautiful bedroom, with a deck outside of it too. Nothing else occurred that night that we were aware of. If we had known what was going on we would not have slept.

21

THE NEXT MORNING, I woke up early, jumped off the bed and nudged T.J. awake.

Hey buddy, what are we going to do? Nice room but I'm sorry we got on this tug.

Me too Jackie Lee, I wish we were home with Captain and everyone. T.J. sighed.

Let's see if we can find out what's going on today or maybe Casey and Peter can get a helicopter to get us off of here. That wasn't a bad idea even if I say so myself, hehe.

T.J. looked at me and as he was about to answer, "T.J., Jackie Lee, what are the two of you barking about?" Casey jumped out of bed and walked over to us. I rolled over and played innocent.

"Casey, I just tried calling the office, the phones are still down all over the ship." Peter got out of bed. "We need to get dressed and take these two out, eat and make a plan."

Casey looked over at him, "I agree Sweetie, let me jump into the shower really quick then we can go." Casey gave me one final pat and got up and walked towards the bathroom.

"Ok, Honey I'm going to make some coffee while you do that." Peter started walking down the stairs.

"Thank you Honey," Casey started shutting the bathroom door but not before I squeezed in.

"Jackie Lee, you just made it, I almost locked you out." Casey laughed.

Casey finished and got dressed. I followed her down to the kitchen and living room area.

Peter gave her a steaming cup of coffee, "Thank you, have you be able to get anything on your phone Peter?"

"No Honey I haven't. The good thing is that Mr. Schim knows our predicament, I hope he comes to our rescue with some help. We really should have gone over our plans with him, but that is hindsight so we have to deal with our reality now." Peter put his coffee cup down.

"Get your leashes boys, are you ready Casey?"

Peter walked over and took the leash out of T.J.'s mouth and clipped it on him. I took mine to Casey and she did the same.

"Let's go, how about the office first." Casey suggested.

"Yes," Peter answered as he unlocked and opened the door.

To our surprise there were two of the boat policemen stationed outside our suite.

"Good morning gentlemen, we didn't know you were here. Thank you for keeping watch. Our dogs need to go out and we need to talk to the Captain and go eat." Peter said.

"We will escort you, my name is Officer McCollum and this is Officer Skinner, we are with the company's official police force and come along on cruises in case of trouble."

"Nice to meet you Officer McCollum and Officer Skinner." Peter shook their hands and so did Casey.

"Thank you for being here." Casey introduced T.J. and me to them too.

We made it down the dog area first as I really had to go and let Casey know. After that we were escorted to the Captain's office.

Captain Jhona rose from his desk, "Good morning Casey and Peter. I see you've met your escorts, we will have 4 in all who will rotate to see over your security until we can reach port. There is no outside communication right now. I am declaring the ship to be under siege of terrorist acts. There will be something done about this as soon as we reach land. I have a private dining room for you and dogs to eat your meals in, there they will have a picnic lunch for you to take to your suite, then you can come back here for dinner. We will make the best of a bad situation and you will be refunded your fares. This is an embarrassment of the worst kind for our ship, please accept my apologies."

"Please, there is nothing for you to apologize for, Captain Jhona! Thank you for your accommodations and security." Casey was overwhelmed by the man's sincerity.

"I have to second my wife's opinion, we are very appreciative." Peter shook his hand.

"Thank you, I'm so glad this will work out, now please go have your meal, there will be food the dogs and they will have food for you to put in your refrigerator for them to have snacks on. We will have what we have down in the dog area put on your deck and it will be cleaned daily so that you can let them out there and not have to go down to the cargo area so often." I have people on that right now. The officers will check out your suite before you enter and stay outside of your suite all of the times."

The Captain is really being nice and doing more for us than I thought would happen. We had a big suite, a hot tub too so we didn't really need to wander around the ship every day. We might get cabin fever if we didn't leave every couple of days, but this cruise wasn't forever. I wonder how long Casey said it was?

I think she said it was like eighteen days, Jackie Lee. That is a long time, hopefully we can fly home.

I agree T.J., oops, Casey is calling. Let's go.

We said goodbye to the Captain and followed the Officers to the room where there was food for us, I was famished!

Peter poured Casey some orange juice, "Honey I have another surprise for you."

"Peter? What is it?" Casey was intrigued.

"Well, we couldn't just go to South America with a treasure map and have no place to stay, so I bought a cute little cottage in Sau Luis, we can rent it out as an Airbnb the rest of the time. Here is a photo of it, this will make a nice getaway for us." Peter handed Casey some photos. I peeked over her shoulder.

"Peter!!! This is adorable! I can't believe it!" Casey got up and hugged Peter."

Peter laughed, "It's ok, I think it was a great investment and there is plenty of room for all of us. We can secure our things while we go on a search for this treasure and Aunt Claire. I love a good treasure hunt!"

Casey sat down and picked up the photo again, "Me too!"

It was wonderful, I saw grass! Then Peter handed her more photos, oh boy! There were waterfalls and a beach nearby too. T.J. and I were going to have so much fun. I just could not wait!

We got back to the room and Casey pulled out the map of where we were to find the treasure.

"I wonder why no one has found this yet, is it a Nazi treasure or something else? Why would my grandfather have this map and not go and find the treasure? If we find it who do we turn it over too?" Casey had so many questions.

"I think we would talk to Mr. Schim and he would tell us, Casey. We will contact him as soon as we get any internet or phone service. At least we have a place to stay when we get there." Peter reminded Casey.

"I know, thank you for being so thoughtful, Peter." Casey threw him a loving glance. "Here it is, let me put it on this table and we can study it some more. I want to take more photos of the map with my phone in case we lose the map."

"That's a really good idea, Casey, I've taken some photos of the map too back at home before we left. I left photos with Baron and Scott just in case we need them. I think we will be pretty ready, it's only these thugs chasing us that are my concern for our safety."

"I agree," Casey sighed and looked out on the deck. "Look, the Captain said he would make a comfortable place for the dogs to take care of their personal business and relax on one of our decks, I'm glad they didn't pick the deck with the view, lol. Come on Jackie Lee and T.J. let's go check out your new area." Casey got up and we followed her outside.

Wow this is nice T.J., we can go anytime and not hold it all night anymore.

Nice, Jackie Lee, think I'll give it a christening. LOL.

"Peter come out here and see T.J. these guys love this deck."

Peter came out with us, "Nice they put all of the furniture on the front part of the deck, it actually is connected Casey, look." Peter walked from where they were to the other part of the deck with doors that came out on the ocean side.

"Casey, why don't we get our dinner and have it out here tonight? It's private and beautiful." Peter leaned over the side. "You can only see our neighbors if you try to."

"Peter, what a marvelous idea. At least we should have some fun, the work begins when we arrive. Hopefully we can get Aunt Claire safely out of harm's way. They want the map in exchange for her or they want the treasure. It's going to take a lot of talent and courage to get her back and not give up the treasure." Casey sat down, "Oh, this is nice." She closed her eyes and seemed to relax for a moment too. I joined her and took a well-deserved snooze, I'm glad I did because remember when I said I felt something was going on we didn't know about?

The hair on the back of my neck stuck way up because we just found out!!!!

22

THERE WAS A RAPID knocking on our cabin door. Peter ran from the deck to the noise.

"What is it?" Peter opened the door.

Officer Skinner was panicked, "We need to get all of you and whatever belongings you can bring, out of here right now!"

"Why?" Peter was astounded.

Casey, T.J. and I ran up behind Peter. "What's going on?" Casey demanded, which was not like her at all. I think she was a bit fed up with the whole situation.

"We have a fire in the engine room, someone started it. We are loading lifeboats until it can be contained. We want everyone safely in them in case the worst happens. Let Officer McCollum and I help you gather a few of your belongings, please?"

Casey backed up and ran over to her laptop, stuffing paperwork in the case and the map back into her purse. Then Peter grabbed a few of their clothes and a toy for each of us.

"Peter! My violin!" Casey stammered.

"It's ok Honey, see? I have it." Peter put his arm around her. "We'll be ok. Now do we have what we need?"

Casey looked around, "I guess so." Then she looked at the officer, "What about water and food?"

"Each lifeboat is filled with both supplies, they are quite large, we are going to be the only ones in yours. Officer McCollum and myself will be with you, do you have what you need?" Asked Officer Skinner, trying to get things moving faster.

"Yes, thank you." Casey softly replied not yet feeling the urgency.

"Let's go then." Peter snapped leashes on both of us. The halls were swamped with people, most appeared to be in a dazed confusion, but we pushed through. Finally, on deck, we saw our lifeboat waiting for us.

"Let me help you in Casey," Peter offered.

"Ok, then let's get the dogs in." Casey took Peter's hand and climbed into the boat. He handed her the suitcase and violin. She placed everything in the shelves on the lifeboat. Then Peter lifted me in, Casey caught me and T.J. was next. Then Peter got in and the two officers after. Other passengers were staring at us dumbfounded why we were the only ones in this lifeboat.

Officer McCollum yelled for our boat to be lowered. This was the real thing.... we were abandoning ship!

It was scary being lowered down into the water. Yipes..... I covered my eyes with my paws. When we were lowered, one of the officers took a sail out of a storage shelf and attached it.

"We need to get well away from the ship in case of sinking. That's why we have the sails attached to all of the lifeboats." Officer Skinner showed Peter how to hook it up.

I looked around, there were a lot of boats out here. I wonder where the bad guys were hiding. I bet they got out too.

All of a sudden there was an explosion from the ship! The front end exploded and the boat started sinking!!!!Debris was flying out in every direction. We were lucky to not get hit by a flying piece of decking as it went past and landed just a few short feet from us.

"It's ok everyone, there was an emergency SOS sent out, but this ship has been sabotaged." Officer McCollum looked at us, "Someone wants something from you and will stop with nothing to get it. They want it bad enough to sacrifice the ship and perhaps some of the passengers."

Peter looked at him grimly, "We have a story to occupy your attention with. I think it's time we filled you in."

Peter and Casey told them what had been happening, what we believed, but they left out the part about the map and a treasure, they even left out that Aunt Claire was kidnapped. I covered my face, I couldn't stand all of this.
I wished I was back with Captain.

See T.J., didn't I say I had a bad feeling? Yikes, why did I have to feel that way. Did I cause it?

Jackie Lee, it isn't your fault, you just have good premonition. You're a detective like Casey in every way.

Thanks T.J., I wonder how long we are going to be on this lifeboat? At least it's equipped with food and water.

That's the way to look at.

T.J. had reminded me of hope.

23

"CASEY," PETER WAS SAYING, "if we get separated for any reason at all, you have the address in your phone of the house we own. Do not attempt to find the treasure on your own, meet me at the house. That will be a much safer place for us, then we can pursue the treasure together. Now, don't look like that, Honey. I'm not saying we will be separated, but it's best to have a plan and be prepared."

"I agree Peter, but it's so much to take in, OH NO!!" Casey was looking at the ship.

"Hold on folks," Officer McCollum commanded. "We're going to try and get out of the way!"

I couldn't believe it, the ship exploded again! Like a bomb it blew it up! Pieces going up in sparks like fireworks. The whole ship was washed in flames. We could feel the heat even though we were now at least 200 yards from it.

"Casey," Peter took her hand, "this is what I mean, they would not blow up the ship and let us go without what they want. Something else is about to happen. I feel it." Peter's voice wavered with concern.

"So, do I, Peter, we must be vigilant. Here," Casey took the map out of her purse, "can you tuck this in T.J.'s collar? I don't feel safe with it on me right now. Besides I could lose my purse in all this muddle."

"Sure, Honey," Peter took the map and rolled in uptight sticking into a waterproof zip liner hidden inside T.J.'s collar, "that should be secure. Casey, you have the map on your phone, make sure that phone is hidden well on you."

"It is Dear," Casey was nervous, I could tell, "it's getting dark, this is where we have to be vigilant."

I was taking it all in, I told T.J. to look in one direction and as I looked the other. The shockwave from the ship blowing up moved us a long distance into the ocean. There were a lot of rafts and survivors, I hoped everyone got out. We looked around and fortunately did not see anyone in the water. We needed to stay bunched as much as possible to help one another and to be more visible for rescue.

"Peter, I'm getting chilled, did you grab anything warm?" Casey was looking around in the bags.

"Here Honey, I stuffed a sweater in this bag." Peter took it out and handed it to Casey.

"Thank you, we might as well get comfortable, no telling when a rescue will come." Casey wrapped her arm around me and buried her face into my fur. "Jackie Lee, we have made it out of worse adventures, I'm sure this will end up ok too." Then she kissed me and I licked her back.

"T.J., come here boy," Casey checked him out too. "you're a good boy, T.J. we will be fine soon buddy." Casey gave him a hug and kiss too, then T.J. licked her back.

"Officer Skinner, do you have any information about survivors?" Peter asked.

"We just got a radio alert, the Captain made it off with the last of the crew, all souls survived and there is military ship rushing towards to save us and drop us off on Algarve. From there a cruise ship will pick us up and we are continuing to South America, everyone's going to be reimbursed for their fares, it's a huge loss, but necessary to keep our good clientele returning. Officer McCollum has made us some hot cocoa to keep ourselves warm this cool night." Officer Skinner handed Casey and Peter a cup each.

"Thank you very much," Casey took a sip. "Hmmm, that's good, do you have anything for the dogs?"

"Yes, thank you Officer McCollum." Peter said when he had swallowed. He scanned the horizon and noted the twinkling of lights on other boats as passengers and crew were settling in for the night.

"Yes, here is some water for the two dogs. Hopefully, we won't have to be out here all night, but we might have to be. We have some food too, so let's relax and try to eat, we might have a rough night ahead of us, if we don't get rescued." Officer McCollum handed Casey, Peter and us some food.

Just as we were finishing a commotion started happening!!! A big ship was approaching, great news, but alongside of it was a submarine and it was headed towards some rafts to the right of us. It stopped, the hatch opened, some rafts were thrown off and men climbed on to them. We watched as they picked up 3 men in a raft and headed back to the sub, but another raft was coming our way! They were shooting guns in the air telling everyone to get down! A bullet just missed me and hit our raft! Officer Skinner grabbed his coat and stuffed it into the hole, while the other officer got a sealer out and tried to place it over the hole. We had lost a bit of air, I was getting seasick. Before I knew what happened a raft zipped by us and Casey was snatched out of our lifeboat! I barked and leaped over the side just making it into the boat that took her. I could hear Peter yelling for help. The raft they were on was just staying afloat and someone needed to get to us before we were abducted and put into the submarine!!!!

24

THIS WAS UNBELIEVABLE, Casey was screaming for help as we zipped past other lifeboats. Someone fired at the raft we were in and it ripped through the side. The man driving the boat cussed in German, shouting orders for another raft from the sub to hurry towards us and help. I looked back, but it was getting too dark to see anything. We got to the sub and someone grabbed me by the neck and put me into the hatch, Casey was forced in after me. We both huddled together.

"What do you want with me?" Casey pleaded.

"You have something that doesn't belong to you, it's a map of something that we need. You will not be let go until we reach South America and you give us the map." The big blond bully commanded. He was built like the Terminator and sounded a bit like him. Not someone to mess with.

"I don't have a map!" Casey cried, "What are you looking for? Where is my Aunt Claire? I don't understand anything happening."

"You won't play that sad card long lady, when we get you to South America. We believe the treasure is in Brazil, but it could be in another area. It is a treasure my ancestor found and hid after WW ll, he was found guilty of killing the Jews and hung without ever revealing where he had buried it. It's been my lifelong dream of recovering it, I have looked everywhere, then you came along and I know your grandfather had some information. I know you must have found something in that cottage of yours. It doesn't have to be this hard! Just give us what we want! Your Aunt Claire will be killed if you resist!"

Casey just shook her head and looked at him defiantly.

"Throw them into a room and leave them there until we get to our destination!" The guy with no name commanded to an underling and stormed off.

Then Casey and I were pushed down a narrow

passageway and shoved into a room.

"Food and water will be provided." The stranger said with no emotion, then he shut the door and locked it.

"Jackie Lee, thank you for coming with me boy." Casey through her arms around me. "I know Peter will find us when we get to South America. Let's try to get some rest, boy, we are going to need it." Casey sat down on the bunk, I jumped up next to her. I snuggled up next to her as she stretched out on the cot. I was in the midst of a dream of a long time ago when about an hour later the door unlocked and food was brought in, a sand box for me. Give me a break! Casey had a bathroom in here, so she was ok, but how embarrassing, I'm not a cat! I think I'll try and not go.

We lived like this day after day, I thought it would never end and so did Casey. Then one morning I looked out the port hole and saw land! Maybe that was South America. Now the fun was about to get better! It took a couple of hours but the sub stopped next to a dock. Someone came into our room to get us. The sun was high overhead, I knew we were in South America, I just didn't know where yet. Casey's hands were cuffed behind her and someone put a choke collar on me, then we were lead away. We walked down the dock and a black car was waiting and we were shoved into the back seat. Looking out the window I could see we were in an old sea town, with fishing nets drying on poles strung out on the upper beach, the streets were well worn cobblestone and the buildings old painted in fading Spanish yellow and green. We didn't drive long before the car slowed and turned into a garage underneath a building. When the car stopped we were marched out into a narrow passageway, up a flight of stairs and into an apartment. The walls were white with stained blotches here and there. There was a rattling air conditioner near the window, which had brown wood shutters. One of the shutters was just hanging from a broken hinge. Casey's hands were taken out of cuffs and I was let go. We were told that we would stay here for the time being. There was food, water, clean clothes for Casey and a high fenced yard for me to use, then the door was shut.

"Jackie Lee, let's try and see what's around us. Listen, I hear a noise." Casey walked over to a bedroom door and opened it. "AUNT CLAIRE!!!!" Casey ran over and hugged her Aunt. "Are you alright? Have they hurt you?"

"Casey and Jackie Lee, am I glad to see the two of you!! I thought you'd never come for me. Where's Peter? Are you here to rescue me?" Aunt Claire had so many questions.

"No, we were abducted, let me tell you the story." Casey sat next to her and for the next hour told Aunt Claire our story.

"Well, that is amazing. So, my dad did know something, we have to find the treasure and never give it to these thugs!" It was fun watching Aunt Claire act so feisty, she didn't act like she was 90 years old. It seems this weather and adventure had made her a young woman again. She had her eyesight, and her wits were still as sharp as ever, and she still could walk, her health seemed a lot better than when we saw her in England.

"We need to make a plan Aunty, I have an

idea." Casey got up and went into the living room. She opened the patio door and we walked outside, Aunt Claire followed me. "Look around this yard, there must be a way for me to make a hole in the fence and we can escape."

"Casey, look over here Dear." Aunt Claire was pointing at the right side of the fence, there was a small hole. I looked through and wagged my tail.

On the other side, there was a yard with no fence and beyond that a sidewalk away from here. Casey moved me out of the way. "I see it Jackie Lee, tonight we make our escape!" Casey stood up. "Good job Aunt Claire, let's go eat and rest, when it gets dark, I'll break that piece of the fence and we get out of here." I followed Aunt Claire and Casey back into the apartment.

"Aunt Claire, how often are you checked on daily?" Casey asked.

"Every day right before supper, someone comes in and checks out the place, replaces food and cleans. They stay about an hour then nothing until the next night. However, with the two of you here, I presume tomorrow during the day we will be visited as well." Aunt Claire opened the fridge and took out some chicken to make a meal. "Casey, there's tomato sauce in the cabinet can you get it please? I'll make a nice Italian dinner for us, they won't suspect our plans that way." Aunt Claire was humming a happy tune. Her spirits have obviously picked up.

"This is going to be fun, you are full of surprises Aunt Claire." Casey handed the tomato sauce to Aunt Claire.

"You don't fall far from the tree either Casey. Look at the adventures and mysteries you and Jackie Lee solve. I would love to hear a story about one of them while we make dinner." Aunt Claire smiled at Casey.

"You've got it! Look, wine! Let me pour us each a glass." Casey handed Aunt Claire her glass. "Cheers."

"Cheers, Dear." Aunt Claire clinked her glass to Casey's.

When I was fed, Aunt Claire was just about to serve their dinner when someone walked in.

"Eating earlier than usual Miss Lane?" The woman asked Aunt Claire.

"Well you know my niece just got here and is hungry. We don't need any food or toiletries today if you want to go." Aunt Claire told the lady.

"My name is Chela Sosa," Chela stuck out her hand to introduce herself to Casey.

"Nice to meet you, I'm Casey and this is Jackie Lee." Casey introduced us.

"Nice to meet you, I'm sorry you had to come here. These are bad men, but my family is being held captive by them and I'm forced to work for them or they will kill my family. I feel so bad for you, if you ever get out is there something you can do to save my family and me?" Chela was pleading. Then she looked around, "I checked there are no listening devices. She looked back at Casey.

"Yes, listen can you help us escape? Casey asked her.

"Yes, if it doesn't look like I did it." Chela answered.

"Where does the road go bchind the house

next door?" Casey pointed next door.

"It leads to the Plaza Pedro, but where will you go if you get to the Plaza?" Chela asked.

Casey hesitated, "I don't know yet, I was just wondering. If we get out we will come for you. If you disappear will they kill your family?"

"I don't know, but I cannot work for these monsters anymore, I am begging for help." Chela pleaded.

"What do you have to do after you leave here?" Casey asked.

"I have to report back to where the men are staying and then they have a room I live in. They keep me like a slave and a prisoner." Now Chela was tearing up.

"Can you get out of that room and escape at night?" Casey asked.

"Maybe, yes, they drink and fall asleep, then I can go. Where do I go?" Chela asked hopefully.

"I have a house that we can hide in until help comes. Meet us by the Cathedral at midnight, is there a way to get transportation out of town that late?" Casey asked.

"No there is not, but my father is a very respected member of this community. I can call one of his good friends to pick us up. They want to help my family from this terror. Other families are being tormented as well." Chela wrote down her father's friend's number and name.

"How can we trust that he will not turn us in, Chela?" Casey asked.

I'm glad she did, because I had the same question.

"He is my father's child hood friend, he works for the Church and is a very holy man. He lives in the Cathedral as its keeper, he will help us." Chela insisted.

"Ok, we will be there at midnight. Please don't come there if you can't get out safely." Casey told her.

"I won't, you have Pedro's number, you tell him about me if I can't make it. He will help you. I must go now, if I'm late they will be mad. Bye." Chela hugged Casey and then Aunt Claire. "Thank you." She said as she closed the door, we heard her walking away.

"Do you trust her Aunt Claire?" Casey

asked.

"Yes, I do, she has been very kind and good to me. I knew her story, I'm glad she decided to share it with you." Aunt Claire placed food down and they had their dinner.

After cleaning up, Aunt Claire turned on the TV for noise. It was dark out and Casey went out back to make an opening. After a few minutes Casey came back in with a smile on her face.

"Ok, we just need to wait for the time to get late. Why don't you take a nap Aunt Claire, we have a busy night and I don't want you to get too tired."

"I'll try Dear, but I'm awfully excited, I think it best for me to sit here with you and talk." Aunt Claire patted the couch for Casey to sit down.

"Ok, let's keep talking and maybe the time will pass quickly." I could tell Casey was anxious, I know I was.

Time moved so slowly, then all of a sudden it was time to go!!! Casey got Aunt Claire up, they grabbed a bag each and we turned out the lights and TV, closing the door behind us. We walked through the opening Casey had made and out onto the side walk. It took fifteen minutes for us make it to the Plaza, then we walked over to the Church.

"Aunt Claire, come here and sit on this bench." Casey had found a seat at the edge of the garden where she could keep an eye out for Chela.

It wasn't too long and a figure came dashing through the shadows. My heart pounded, but with relief it was Chela and not someone else.

"I made it and so did you!" Chela whispered. "I called my dad's friend, follow me, he is waiting for us."

Casey helped Aunt Claire up and we followed Chela around the back of the Cathedral.

"Hi, Pedro, thank you, here are my friends." Chela walked over and hugged her friend.

"Hello my little one, oh, nice to meet you." Chela introduced us and shook his hand.

"Well, hurry, we must go while it is late." We followed Pedro to his car. We got in and Casey gave him the address.

"Oh, that is a nice area, it is 4 hours from here, we had better get going, I have tomorrow off so it doesn't matter when I return, but we don't want to be found out." Pedro drove out of the Plaza and into the lush green country. I was tired and fell asleep, Aunt Claire did too, but I heard Casey talking to Pedro and Chela.

"There it is!" Casey pointed, "Oh, it's adorable! My husband bought this little house for us. Pedro, you must stay until daylight and get some rest and food. You said you were off, right?"

"Yes, that would be nice, is there some place to hide my car?" Pedro asked.

"There is no garage, but just right over there under those trees, the car and house cannot be seen from the road." Casey pointed to the parking spot.

Pedro eased his car to the spot and stopped.

I could hear Chela give a big sigh of relief.

"I can't believe this is happening, I know they will tear up the town looking for us. I feel that we can be safe here though. Thank you." Chela reached over and squeezed Casey's hand.

"Your welcome, thank you for helping us too. Let's get out and go inside." Casey opened her door, I jumped out and then Pedro helped Aunt Claire out.

Casey walked up onto the patio and found a key under a planter by the glass doors. She took out her cell phone and used it for light to put the key into the lock. We followed her in. Peter had great taste, I fell in love with this place! Too bad it wasn't in America, I was homesick. There were three bedrooms, Pedro and Chela got the room with twin beds overlooking the garden, Aunt Claire got the room with a double bed and Casey and I got the master bedroom with a big window overlooking the garden. The walls were brick, and the floors had decretive tile patterns like a mosaic. This place was gorgeous. I knew Casey was impressed too. All of us went to sleep right away. It had been a very hard week.

****

We assumed Peter and T.J. were on a cruiser coming our way, but knowing Peter, he hired a jet to get him to us sooner. He loved Casey with a passion I couldn't understand. He would be devastated if anything ever happened to her. I knew Casey felt the same way about him, she was hesitant to marry him because of her feelings for an old boyfriend. She knew in her heart that she had made the right decision though and once this was over with we could all go home and have a normal life. Maybe they would have a kid for T.J. and me to play with, that would be fun, but I wasn't sure Casey was ready for that yet. Maybe someday.

****

The sun rose and the house brightened up. I opened up my eyes to see if Casey was awake. She was stirring so I went over and licked her. I needed to go out.

"Good morning Jackie Lee, let's get up." Casey jumped up and put on a robe that was in the closet. In fact, Peter had someone deliver clothes for Casey, wow! I was impressed. Anyway, she put on her robe, put on some flip flops and went to the garden doors, opened them up for me to go out. Then she went in and made coffee for everyone.

https://www.airbnb.com/rooms/9522432

By the time Chela, Aunt Claire and Pedro were up, Casey had fruit, meats, cheese, coffee, juice and my food out ready for everyone. Casey had taken her shower and changed into a long sundress, she looked pretty. The only thing missing was Peter.

I could not wait for T.J. and Peter to arrive!!!!! Hopefully Peter would surprise us and get here sooner than later. Until then we were going to relax and have some down time. After breakfast, Chela cleaned up, Casey gave her a dress to wear and we walked down to the beach and waterfalls. Casey and Peter would have no problem making this an Airbnb at all.

I think I could get used to living here....at least for part of the year. Then maybe if we survived this we could come back from time to time. After playing in the water and having the time of my life, Casey called me out and we walked back up to the house. I lounged out under a tree, Pedro stayed most of the day and late in the afternoon he decided to get back, he would let us know of anything suspicious.

"I am sure they are looking everywhere for you, Chela and our friends too. I will pray that your family is safe, we will be in touch. I am off in a week, if any of you need anything, Chela can call me, or you can Casey." After hugs he got into his car and drove away.

"Well, what should we do?" Casey asked. "How about a game of cards? I'll make some ice tea and bring out snacks."

"I'll help you," Chela chimed in.

"I'll sit here if you don't mind and wait for you two to come back." Aunt Claire found a comfortable chair and looked out into the garden. I could see her living here. I could see us living here, I loved it! We couldn't go into town though, too dangerous right now.

The days flew by, I could tell Casey was getting restless worrying about Peter. We were having an amazing vacation, I missed Captain too though, hopefully T.J. would be here soon. I sighed, Casey looked at me.

"I'm feeling the same way, boy. Hopefully, Peter will call or be here any day now." Casey rubbed my head.

Casey's phone rang, she ran inside, it was charging and grabbed it. "Hello."

"Yes, oh no, they don't suspect you or Father of helping do they? Good, ok, thank you for letting us know. Chela is down on the beach; do you want her to call you? No, ok, keep in touch, thank you."

"Jackie Lee, that was Pedro, the men have been frantically looking for us. Scary business, I'm so glad we are hiding here."

I thumped my tail, where was Peter?????? Then to answer my question a cab pulled up! Casey ran outside, Peter got out first, then T.J. Casey was in Peter's arms before I even got there. Peter paid the cab driver and gave me a hug.

"Honey, I'm so glad you made it here, I love this place!" Casey was so excited.

"It's beautiful, I'm so happy you love it Casey. I love you so much. It hurts. You can't conceive how worried I was about you. Let's sit down and you can tell me all about your story." Peter led her onto the porch.

"Peter, there is a young girl who helped us, she is here with us. Her family is being held by these men and she escaped to help us get here, her name is Chela, she is down at the beach right now." Casey pointed towards the beach. "Let me get you some lemonade and we can sit here and talk, the dogs can run around." Casey ran inside and came out with two glasses of chilled lemonade.

"What happened to you and Jackie Lee?" Peter wanted to know." Where is Aunt Claire?"

"She will be right out, she was taking a nap. She is an amazing woman Peter. You should have seen us escaping!" Casey laughed.

Peter laughed too, "I wish I could have."

"What happened to you?" Casey asked.

"We were rescued right after you were abducted. Then taken to a coastal city in France. I didn't wait for the cruise ship, I hired a plane, but I had to wait a week to get one. That is why I was delayed. I could not continue a cruise without you." He leaned over and kissed Casey.

"Good, I missed you. Here comes Chela now." Casey stood up.

"Chela, come here, my husband, Peter arrived."

"Hello," Chela ran over to shake Peter's hand. "Your kind wife saved me, I love your house."

"I'm glad they met you, I believe Casey is indebted to you for your help too. We will somehow resolve this. I just need a day or two to rest and make some plans with Casey. Here is Aunt Claire. Excuse me Chela, please sit down." Peter got up and helped Aunt Claire to a seat.

"It's very nice to see you, Peter." Aunt Claire said smiling.

"It's very nice to see you too." Peter hugged her.

Casey stood up, "Anyone for lemonade?"

"Yes, I'll go get it." Chela jumped up. "Aunt Claire, do you want any?"

"Yes please." Aunt Claire replied. "Ok, when does our next adventure begin?" Aunt Claire asked Peter.

Everyone laughed, Claire placed the glasses out and the lemonade pitcher on the table.

"I have a map, we need to look at it and decide where this treasure is hidden." Peter reached into T.J.'s collar and pulled out a map. He placed it on the table for all to look at it.

That was clever T.J. hiding a map in your collar! I wagged my tail.

I'm just glad we found you! T.J. barked.

Chela traced it with her finger. "This leads below the Cathedral, she looked at Peter. There are tombs down there, could they be under the tombs or hidden someplace else?"

"Good questions," Casey looked at the map too. "How should we go about this? I don't think it's safe for all of us go. This is a safe hideout, I think Peter and I should go, you two should stay here in case anything happens to us."

"I like that plan," Aunt Claire agreed.

"Hmm, I think I do too," Chela said, "it would be fun to find treasure though!"

"It's just maybe the first time, you could stay with Aunt Claire to keep her company. Then we can arrange something else. We need to see how it feels, we can't risk your life getting you caught up into our mess when your family is in so much danger." Casey pointed out.

"I know you're right, I just want some excitement in my life." Chela sighed.

Casey laughed, "You will have plenty of time for excitement, and meeting boys, how old are you?"

"I'm 18." Chela said proudly.

"That is so young." Aunt Claire laughed, "I'm 90."

"What? You look amazing!" Chela was shocked.

"Thank you, Chela, I like that young people are so polite." Aunt Claire smiled.

"I would like to see my house." Peter stood up. "My wife and I will be back shortly, excuse us." Peter took Casey's hand.

Peter grabbed his bag, and my violin then they walked into the house.

Of course, T.J. and I followed. I had really missed T.J.

"This is really cute, Casey, I'm glad I found such a good buy, we will be able to rent this out with no problem if we want to. Do we want to? I like it here?" Peter took her into his arms and they kissed.

Casey took Peter's hand and they went through the bedrooms, Casey showing him everything. The bathroom is what Casey went on about.

"See Peter," Casey opened up the bathroom door. A double sink vanity in front of a large mirror was next to the shower built for two. The shower had two folding lounge chairs for lying on when the shower's steam room unit was in use.

"Yes, I like it, very tastefully done. Where is our room? I want to change." Peter asked.

"Right here, Honey." Casey opened the

door and led him in. I'll give you a moment, do you want to shower?"

"Yes, that would be nice. I'm so relieved to be here, tomorrow let's make a plan about our treasure hunt, Casey."

"Yes, tomorrow, I'll go start dinner." Casey blew him a kiss, but Peter caught her and held her tight. "I've missed you so much, I couldn't imagine my life without you Casey. I'm so blessed and lucky you landed on my island."

Casey had to laugh at that one. "I'm the lucky one. You saved me more than once. Go take your shower." She shoved him into the bathroom and closed the door. As Casey walked away I noticed she was smiling. I was pretty happy myself. WOOF!

After dinner that night, the map was brought out again, "So, you think Chela, that this leads to someplace under or by the Cathedral De Sao Luis, in Maranhao, Brazil? This is what you think?" Peter asked her the question twice.

"Yes, I believe it is, I have lived here my whole life. It has to be there, this points to the

Plaza, the Cathedral De Sao Luis is the biggest building there." Chela was tracing her finger over the dots.

"Peter, we must call Mr. Schim in the morning. He will be worried sick about us. We need to call Baron, Scott, Robert and Jack too. I'm sure they are worried, concerned and curious about what is happening." Casey emphasized.

"You're right, we do need to do that. Germany is 5 hours ahead of us and England is 4 hours ahead of us. I say it's too late tonight, we will do it first thing in the morning. I had this place filled with food and clothes, Chela do you have enough clothes? How about you Aunt Claire?" Peter inquired, being the polite and thoughtful person I knew him to be.

"I brought a few items with me, but I didn't want to take a lot, not that I had a lot, but I didn't want it to look like I ran away. I could use some more clothes, Peter, if it isn't too much trouble?" Chela was embarrassed asking.

"No problem, I will get a car delivered tomorrow as well. We will go shopping, not in

Sau Luis, but a closer town and buy some clothes. Aunt Claire, how about you?" Peter asked.

"I need some clothes, I was taken from home with nothing. I would like to burn the things they gave me, this whole thing was just unnecessary and greedy, if you want my opinion." Aunt Claire huffed.

Peter laughed affectionately, "I couldn't agree more, Aunt Claire, well said."

"Yes, I agree as well. This is all about greed, I know my grandfather must have felt the same way. I wonder why he had the map but never acted on it?" Casey asked Aunt Claire.

"I presume his new wife and family must be kept in the dark. How could he have gone to South America after he married your grandmother, Casey? It wouldn't be possible, perhaps he just didn't care anymore, the war was over. He had a new family to care for. We just will never know for sure what he was thinking. My father was a very private person, it's amazing he took my mother, brother and myself to Brazil with him, when he was working as a spy. I wish we could get the whole story, but we can only use our imagination and make a story."

Wow, that was a lot of talking for Aunt Claire, I was impressed, I could tell the others were as well. Yes, I was eavesdropping.

"You're right Aunt Claire, I would like to have known my father and mother. I am sure now that they were murdered because of this hidden treasure. Someone must have thought my dad knew something or perhaps my dad was also MI-5?" Casey asked.

"I don't think he was MI-5, Casey, I believe he was in the spy business, however, hmmmmm……" Aunt Claire was thinking.

"What is it Aunt Claire?" Peter asked.

"I just had a thought about one time when my dad met my brother and myself, after he had remarried. He told me that his son was growing up to be just like him and it scared him. I never knew what he meant, he never offered to tell me and I didn't dare ask. Now I wish I had asked, I never met my half-brother, your father, Casey." Aunt Claire shook her head in sadness.

"It's ok, Aunt Claire," Casey comforted her, "how could you have known what the future was to bring? I'm just so happy you found me!" Casey got up and put her arms around Aunt Claire, giving her a reassuring hug.

"Thank you Casey for coming into my life, I love you." Aunt Claire whispered to Casey.

"You're welcome, thank you too." Casey replied, kissing her cheek.

"You're going to make me cry." Said Chela, "I'm so happy you found me. I pray my family is going to be ok."

"That is why Mr. Shim must be informed, he will have agents here that can help. I will tell him about your family. They will be found and saved I am sure of it." Peter assured her.

Chela smiled, "Thank you."

"Let's see what tomorrow brings, shall we? I'm tired, I need to sleep." Peter said getting up. "Casey are you coming now or staying up?"

"I'll be right there after I let the dogs out, Honey." Casey rose from the table and kissed Peter. "Night sweetheart."

"Night everyone." Peter left.

"Good night," Chela yelled after him. "Thank you, Casey."

"You are so welcome, why don't you get ready for bed now? Aunt Claire do you need anything before retiring?" Casey asked.

"I need a shower, so goodnight." Chela got up and left.

"I'm fine Casey, thank you." Aunt Claire picked up her book. "I'm going to bed to read for a bit. I'll see you in the morning."

"Good night." Casey then turned to T.J. and me. "Let's go out boys." Casey opened the door and went out with us.

It was a beautiful warm night; little lights were lit in the garden. What a paradise this was, hopefully no bad guys would find us here. Yikes, what a thought!

The next morning was busy, the phone calls were made. Mr. Schim had agents, they were on the way to find the Nazi thugs and Chela's family. He cautioned Casey and Peter to be careful looking for the treasure and to contact him as soon as it was found. Then they got Baron and the gang on the phone. I got to talk to

Captain, he wasn't happy being left in England and wished he was here.

25

I NUDGED CASEY, she looked down at me, "What is it Jackie Lee?" Casey appeared confused.

I looked across the street, Casey followed my gaze.

"Peter, look over there! I think we are being watched!" Casey grabbed her purse.

Peter looked across the street. Two unscrupulous and threatening looking persons were peering at them while trying to look inconspicuous. "Yes, I believe you're right. Let's everyone slowly get up. We are going to the car and then we are going to lose them!" Peter left money on the table with the bill and grabbed T.J.'s leash, Casey had Aunt Claire up and attached me to a leash too.

We walked like nothing was happening but as soon as we got into the car, Peter sped out of town. He headed out away from our house. We took the roadway along the waterfront. we drove by water and to another town. I peered back and a car was erratically following us, Peter had to lose them now. The car pulled up next to us and one of the thugs pointed a handgun and fired into our car. Peter stepped on the gas. Pushing the car upwards of 80 kph as we went winding down the narrow road. The bullet blew out our back window as it whizzed by Aunt Claire in the back seat. Aunt Claire screamed.

"Are you doing ok back there?" Peter cried out!

"Yes, just scared, go Peter turn off up there!" Aunt Claire pointed to another windy road.

Instead Peter braked hard while turning the wheel and swung the car around and went back towards the pursuers.

"What are you doing?" Casey cried out grabbing the dashboard to avoid bouncing wildly and possibly bumping Peter.

"Everyone duck!" Peter shouted.

I jumped on Aunt Claire and got her down,

Chela was on the floor, T.J. was on her. Peter sped by, they shot again but they were going in the wrong direction and missed us. Then Peter turned off going up a rough mountain road. Well, not the kind we find in the US, but this was a mountain in Brazil. We didn't go far when we reached a waterfall. Peter took a little used dirt road and barely squeezed the car under the falls. We were certain no one could see us unless they knew to look behind the falls. All of us held our breath. 20 minutes later the car chasing us zoomed by and missed us. Peter waited for the dust to settle, then got us clear of the waterfall and went back the way we came, he took us home. Fortunately, no one was following us. Peter hid the car and everyone got out. When we arrived home. We were exhausted and frightened.

"I'm shaken to the core." Aunt Claire said, "I don't want any more of this. I'm staying put, right here. Let's find this treasure and go home."

"Aunt Claire, let me make you some tea. Better yet let me make everyone some tea, we need to ease our rattled nerves." Casey unlocked the porch door and Aunt Claire went inside. Casey told T.J. and me to come in too. When all of us had calmed down, and we were sitting around the kitchen table, Peter called Mr. Schim again.

"I couldn't reach him, but left a message." Peter said hanging up.

"That's ok, Honey, I think we need to lay low tomorrow and for a few days." Casey said.

"I agree, they were in the town where our house is. I hope they don't find us here. I'm really disturbed that this happened. They must now know that we are staying nearby. Perhaps they traced the house bill of sale with our names and quickly deduced we were staying there. They may have been watching, waiting for the right moment to make a move. We may not be safe here much longer. They saw you too Chela, that can't be good news for your family." Peter was indeed worried.

"There is nothing my family knows and my father's friend, Pedro is ok or he would have called again. He called yesterday and said the Priest was questioned but then the men left.

How big of an operation is this do you think, Peter?" Chela asked.

"It must be international, they were bothering us in England, on the sea and now here, Mr. Schim in Germany is on to them too. Disgusting, we need to quickly find that treasure and get this finished." Peter did indeed look disgusted.

I was tired of this and so was T.J. I looked at him.

Want to go down to the waterfalls, buddy?

T.J. looked at me and wagged his tail, them looked at Peter.

"Ha, I think the dogs want to go and play a bit. It might be a good idea. Who is up for it?" Peter stood up.

"I'm ready." Casey said, "Let me go change."

"I'm going to rest in my room and read," Aunt Claire stated.

"I'll go with you, let me put on some of my new clothes." Chela got up and grabbed her bags then went to her room.

I waited with T.J. and Peter for the girls to

come back, when they did we made our way down to the falls. It was beautiful!

http://googleshortener.com/I96MCisP

A much-needed rest was needed after the harrowing time we had in town. I didn't think we would be going to town anytime too soon. We are 4 hours from Sao Luis, how could they find us here? They must have just been on a fishing expedition. I was excited to see what could be so special about the hidden treasure. I was going to find out soon.

26

WE RESTED THE next day, but the day after Peter was itching to get started. After breakfast Peter announced our itinerary.

"Today we will go on a scouting expedition, just to test the water. Aunt Claire, you and Chela need to stay here. Stay inside and avoid being in front of the windows. If anyone comes up to the house, hide and do not answer the door. I want you inside the house locked up tight. We need T.J. and Jackie Lee to help us so you won't have a dog, there will be no car for anyone to think that you are home. If anything should happen to us, here is Mr. Schim's number, and Baron's number, call them and then call your friend Pedro. Trust no one else and be brave." Peter hugged Aunt Claire, she was frightened and crying.

"Aunt Claire, we will be ok, we need to get going or we will get home too late. Chela, take care of her, ok?" Casey asked.

"Of course, I will, we have the contact numbers and we can play cards or read. It will feel good to relax. Just be careful, please????" Chela was very cute, Casey went over and hugged her.

"Yes, we will, perhaps we will have a great story to tell you when we return." Casey turned towards Peter.

"I'm ready, are you?"

"Yes, Casey, I am. Come on dogs, we need to drop off the rental and get another one without a broken window. Plus, a different car will be better to throw them off our scent." Peter grabbed the leashes, water, and keys.

Casey said goodbye again and locked all of the doors, then we drove off. Peter drove us all the way to Arari, we were on MA-222, about a fourth of the way to Sao Luis. It was a long drive, but gave us time to review our plan and get ready to work hard. We arrived at noon, Peter rented a car with tinted windows, it was a

Mercedes and blended right in with other cars on the road. He drove us around the Plaza, the Cathedral was unbelievably huge, it is a beautiful example of early Portuguese architecture. Casey studied the map.

"Let's park on a side street and go into the Cathedral, there should be an entrance from outside to the tombs beneath the church, but maybe there is a way from inside. The outside would be locked, I don't want to bother the priest or Pedro if we can help it." Casey rolled up the map and stuck it in her jacket.

"I agree, ok, let's park here." Peter parked the car under a tree south of the Cathedral. "Let me check out the area, while you guys stay in here for a minute."

Peter came back a few minutes later after a casual reconnaissance of the area. "We are all clear, let's go."

I jumped out and stuck to Casey like glue, we made our way to a back door of the Cathedral. There were many people inside taking photos of the gorgeous carvings, stained glass windows, and statues. We hid behind a statue so Peter and Casey could get a good look around. There were statues all over and marble columns too.

"Over there, Casey," Peter whispered, "I see a door it isn't like the other doors, this one looks more private."

"Ok, let's go." Casey whispered back. I followed her, she tried the door, it was locked.

"I have a pick," Casey took it out of her pocket, she stuck it in the lock, gave it a few twists and turns and it popped.

"Handy to have a wife that break into things," Peter chuckled softly. Casey grinned at him.

We cautiously and silently went through the door and Peter quietly closed it behind us. There were stairs going down and it was dark so we had no idea how far down they went. Casey took out her phone to use as a light. It helped with seeing a few steps ahead but the light was too weak to penetrate any farther. We carefully walked down the alabaster steps. When we got to the bottom, Peter found a light switch. It sure would have been nice to have a switch at the top of the stairs. There were ten very old tombs, we walked around each of them. The last tomb looked different. It was newer looking and had a dissimilar style from the rest. Casey put her hands all around the side and found something.

"A switch," she said.

Casey flipped it and the tomb creaked and groaned as it sluggishly moved, below that stairs appeared. Casey looked suspiciously at Peter.

"Let me go first Casey." If there was another light switch, it eluded us. After borrowing Casey's phone, Peter took the lead, we followed. We got down to the end of the stairs and there were more doors. "Where is the bloody light switch?" You could tell Peter was getting frustrated when he says "bloody". Peter doesn't get upset very often.

"Which door should we try first?" Casey thought out loud. Peter didn't hear her, he was too occupied.

I was thinking, how about closing that opening above us and my thoughts must have transferred to Casey, because she said the same to Peter. That got his attention.

"Good idea," Peter walked over to the bottom of the stairs and felt around the walls, he found a hidden lever and we heard the tomb closing.

"Peter, if there is a switch of some kind, then someone knows about this!!!" Casey stated the exact facts I thought was obvious.

"Casey, those tombs are very very old, the switch was rusty and nearly frozen in position. It's also dusty down here. I don't think anyone alive knows about this.

"Ok, let's try that door over there." Casey pointed to the third door on the end barely illuminated by her phone light.

Peter walked over, "I'm afraid 'door number 3' is locked," he looked back at Casey.

She walked over and did her thing. After picking the lock the door creaked open. She stuck her phone inside and looked around. "Nothing here," she said. "Let's try door number 2."

Casey went over and picked open that lock, the door didn't budge. Peter leaned on it and together they got it to move. When I got inside I could not believe my eyes. NOTHING! Except another door opening in the floor. This is turning into a maze.

Sooooo, Peter lifted the cover and there were more stairs. Now I was getting a bit claustrophobic, we were going deep, deep into the earth. I followed reluctantly, it was worth it though!

"Peter!! Look at this!" Casey pointed to an engraved statue. THE PROPERTY OF THE KNIGHTS TEMPLAR.

"Good grief! This is stolen from the Knights Templar. There aren't any of them around anymore, so who would get this?" Peter asked. I didn't know and neither did Casey.

Casey found some jewelry, then she picked up a big necklace, it had a clock on it or something like a clock.

"Peter, look at this." Casey showed him.

"Casey, this has a dial on it with a switch, it has the year 1184 on it!" Peter looked at her. "Is it a time travel device?"

Casey took it back and examined it, "Sure could be, do you see anything else like this?"

She looked around the room. There were paintings, gold nuggets, and more jewelry, was there another matching necklace? I looked and couldn't find one.

"There must be more treasure someplace, but this is the one my grandfather was after. I can't explain my feelings right now, Peter." Casey closed her eyes.

"SHHH, did you hear that?" Peter ran up and put the cover back on top of the stairs, then joined us.

"Someone is up in the tombs Peter." Casey was nervous, so was I.

"No one saw us, I'm sure of it. Listen." Peter tried to listen. There was shouting up above. We could hear the priest yelling at someone telling them to get away from the tombs. They were bashing the tops of them!!!!

"Casey, we're trapped here. Unless there is an exit out of this maze we can't get out, we must be quiet."

We heard a gunshot! "Oh no! They shot the priest!" Casey was panicking.

"Hurry, Casey, we're trapped, they're outside." Peter urged her to try the necklace she had found.

Someone was coming down closer to us. "Everyone get very close to me. I'm going to put this necklace on and press the dial." Casey grabbed the necklace.

The door above was being removed!
All of a sudden, a light spread out in a circle around us! We disappeared as the door above us opened and they saw us vanish! We were traveling through time!!!!!

"Hang on Casey," Peter called.

"You too, the dogs are with us, look!" Casey tried to reach out to me but I could not get to her and all of a sudden, we landed. Boom.
I looked around, where were we?
Casey picked herself up and checked me over, Peter was already checking out T.J.

"We had better find out what century we are in and find shelter, Cascy." Peter hugged her closely.

"My exact sentiments." Casey replied.

We walked down a dirt road watching for anyone to approach us.

"Hurry, hide!" Peter grabbed Casey and all of us hid behind some bushes.

I held my breath, and so did T.J., we didn't dare bark.

There were Knights on horses riding down the road, they had the Templar Cross on their shields. What they were doing or where they were going was not our concern. We were here to find out why the Knights had left treasure in Brazil for us to find many centuries later and to escape the threat of being shot by the people that shot the priest.

They passed by and all of us let out a sigh of relief.

"Casey, do you still have the necklace?" Peter asked worriedly.

"Yes, Honey." Casey pulled the chain out of her shirt, "see, hidden."

"Good, we might want to go back sooner than later."

I second that one, let's go!!!! I barked. Casey hushed me.

T.J. whimpered and Casey hugged him, "It's ok, we will go back soon. Let's explore."

Exploring was fun if you knew where and when your next meal was coming. This was a bit scary to say the least. It was getting dark and we had nowhere to go.

27

"HELLO, IS THAT YOU Jackie Lee?" A voice asked.

I looked around, it was pitch dark in this cave, did someone call my name or is my active imagination running away again taking me with it?

Casey heard it too, "Who's there?" she calmly asked the voice.

Then a big white dragon came forward whose bulk almost filled the cave. "Don't be afraid, but I think I know you. Do you know Gunther?"

"Yes, we helped Sophia and Kanani a few years ago rescue Gunther's family from northern Scotland, how did you know?" Casey was curious, so was everyone clse.

"My name is Emmorous, I was a baby when we got rescued by Gunther. I live in Camelot now, I'm out on patrol. There has been much unrest in the area bordering on chaos and anarchy."

"I remember you! I'm Casey and this is Jackie Lee, I can't believe you remembered his name you were so young. This is my husband, Peter and our other dog, T.J." Casey introduced us by pointing to each of us as she spoke.

"He he, imagine that. What are you doing here in my cave tonight?" Emmorous asked.

"It's an amazing story, we found the Templar Treasure that was stolen from them, someone was after us and we found this necklace that took us back in time." Casey pulled out her necklace for him to see.

"I see, like I said there is much unrest in the Kingdom." Emmorous informed us again.

"Where is Sophia right now, do you know?" Casey asked.

"Sophia, Kanani, and some knights are getting ready to go on a quest to find the Holy Grail or the Ten Commandments." He informed us.

"UM, excuse me," Peter interrupted, "I have something to confess." He pulled out a cup.

"Casey, while you were looking at the jewelry, I found some religious articles and this cup was among the artifacts. When we heard the intruders, I put it in my knapsack and the next thing we were here. I couldn't show you or put it back, I'm sure there was a lot more hidden there as well."

"Let me take a closer look at that." Emmorous peered at the cup. "It's an average sized unpretentious metal cup shaped like a wine glass. It has a crude design etched or scratched on the outside that is well worn and hard to distinguish. It could be the cup they are looking for. Why don't I take you to Camelot in the morning, we can catch them before they leave? King Arthur can see this and tell us about it. I'm sure you have an amazing story to tell all of us. For now, I will watch over you as you sleep tonight." Emmorous backed up giving us room to spread out and sleep. "Good night."

"Good night Emmorous, thank you," Casey and Peter both said, then Casey looked at Peter.

"I bet there was more treasure as precious as this in that room. I hope those awful men didn't get in there and take anything. This is just amazing." Casey held the cup and looked at it as best she could in the dim light from her phone.

"Well, I guess I get to meet the famous Sophia and Kanani tomorrow, Gunther the dragon too. I can't believe this treasure hunt led us here." Peter could not stop shaking his head in disbelief.

I looked at T.J. We get to see Kanani, she is a great looking German Shepherd and my friend, I'll be happy for you to have her as a friend too.

I've heard about your trip to Camelot, I can't believe I get to go now too!!! T.J. wagged his tail and spun around.

"T.J., Jackie Lee, we must be quiet and get some sleep, we might be safe from the Nazi hunters but there are other dangers here. Dangers we are not aware of, because in our time we don't have them." Peter put his arm around T.J.

I walked over and snuggled with Casey.

The sun rose before I had enough shut eye, Emmorous was good to his word, he found some berries for us to eat. We were just cleaning up when we heard a noise. Peter peeked out of the cave, then backed up with his finger on his lips. He sat down next to us and whispered, "I can't believe what I just saw. The guys chasing us just showed up. There must have been another necklace. I think they are determined to get this cup I found." Then he looked at Emmorous. "How can you get us out of here?"

"There's a back entrance to this cave, follow me." Emmorous replied, he turned to take another passage.

We got to the end of it and walked into the burned down castle.

Emmorous crouched down, "Get on me."

Peter helped Casey up, then he helped us get up, when he climbed Aboard. Each of them had a firm grip on one of us with one hand and the dragon with the other.

"Here we go!!!" Emmorous stated. His enormous wings stretched out, flapped a couple of times then we soared up into the air and looked down below. We had just sailed over the people following us, there were two of them. They looked astounded that we were on a dragon and they couldn't do anything about it. They would have no idea where we were going and each moment they were out an about exposed them to the danger of being discovered. We now had a definite advantage. They would have no choice but to return to our home time. Peter had an idea.

"Casey," Peter shouted, so she could hear him. "We must get those guys arrested over here, maybe the Knights of Camelot can get them!"

"Yes, a grand idea! Look at the countryside, Peter! Isn't it stunning? It's changed so much in our time, here it is still so uninhabited and pristine."

"Yes, it is beautiful; I'm still awing at the shock of riding a real dragon!" Peter laughed.

We covered the distance pretty quickly, dragons can fly fast. When Camelot came into view, I got so excited!!!
Emmorous landed next to a cave behind Sophia's house. Gunther came out to greet Emmorous and see who we were. He was amazed upon seeing that his good friends had come for a visit.

"My my, I never thought we would see the likes of you ever again Casey Lane and Jackie Lee. You brought another person and German Shepherd with you too. What do we owe this surprise to?" Gunther was elated upon seeing us.

"Gunther, I found your friends, they are being pursued by evil men and I brought them here." Emmorous told his fellow dragon.

"Hi Gunther, it's so good to see you too." Casey slid off Emmorous and went over giving Gunther a kiss on his nose.

"Aww, I like that. We need to go get Sophia, she is getting ready to leave. Follow me." Gunther rose up and walked towards a house.

"Sophia!" Gunther called.

A door opened up and Sophia stepped outside. She looked at Gunther then behind him and jumped up and down, then ran over to Casey and hugged her.

"I can't believe you're here! How did you get here? What's going on? Who is this handsome man and dog with you? Hi Jackie Lee. Kanani! Come on girl, Jackie Lee is here!" Sophia was talking a mile a minute.

"I'm just so happy to see you Sophia, it's a long story, but we found a treasure including a time travel necklace and then Emmorous found us." Casey put her arm around her friend. "This is my handsome husband, Peter and his dog, T.J."

Sophia shook Peter's hand, "It's great to meet you." Then she looked at T.J., "Hi buddy, welcome to my home and time."

T.J. barked and wagged his tail.

Then Kanani came bounding outside. There was plenty of sniffing, barking, chasing and greeting.

"Emmorous, thank you for bringing my friends, Gunther I'll see you soon."

"Ok, bye Sophia." Emmorous said.

"I'll be waiting here Sophia." Gunther said.

Sophia turned to us. "Come into my home, I'm packing for a quest that we are about to leave on today." Sophia opened her door for us to enter.

It was a cute little house, cobblestone floors, one bedroom, then a studio with Sophia's paintings and her writing. Compared to the 21st century standards this was like minimalist living. Just the essentials for furniture, a table, some chairs, and a bed platform. The house was open, nothing was separating the living space from the kitchen. Only the bathroom and bedroom had doors.

"About that quest, Sophia. Peter found something very interesting. Can you show her Peter?" Casey asked.

Peter put his bag down and pulled out the cup.

Sophia's eyes got huge, "Oh, this might be the Holy Grail! Lamorak, my knight should be here soon. We can take this to King Arthur, only then will we know if it is the real cup or not." Sophia put it on the table. "If it isn't the real cup, it's still gorgeous. Where did you find it?"

"We found it hidden underneath the tombs in a church in Brazil. It was from the Knights Templar treasures that were stolen during WWll by the Nazi's and hidden in Brazil. We are still being pursued by these horrid people. Emmorous got us out of harm's way just in time. The men followed us through time, somehow. We got here with this necklace." Casey pulled it out from under her shirt. It was hanging around her neck.

"That's also elegant Casey. Wow, this is amazing." Sophia walked over to the door and opened it. Looking outside she saw someone and waved. Then looking back at us, she said, "Lamorak is on his way now. I think you'll like him Peter."

"Hi Honey." Sophia hugged Lamorak. "I have a surprise for you. Come in and meet my friends."

"What friends my dear, are you packed?" Lamorak asked.

"Yes, but Peter, Casey's husband has found something. Please take a look." Lamorak held her hand as they approached the table.

Introductions were made and Lamorak looked the cup over. "This looks very real, only one person will know, Merlin! We must find him before this quest starts and I need to let King Arthur know as well. We must get going." Lamorak handed the cup to Peter. "Please accompany me." He took Sophia's hand and we followed him to the castle. It wasn't a very long walk, we went over a bridge and entered the town in the castle, then followed Lamorak to a door. He knocked on it, the door opened and an older man with white hair and a long white beard appeared.

"Casey!" Merlin stepped outside his door and hugged her. "What is this visit about? Look here, you brought a friend and another German Shepherd. Come in everyone. Lamorak, Sophia, nice to see you. Please, everyone have a seat."

"Merlin, it's great seeing you as well. We came here by accident, but I'm glad we did. My husband, Peter, has something to show you." Casey asked Peter to open his bag.

Peter took out the cup and handed it to Merlin.

"Hmm, hmmm," Merlin looked at it from top to bottom and back again. "There is a test I can give it. Lamorak please go get Arthur and let him know what I'm doing and what is going on."

Lamorak stood up, "Yes, I will return after I talk to him. Bye everyone."

"Bye Lamorak, hurry back please." Sophia replied.

Merlin got up and walked over to his wooden table with all sorts of herbs and colorful liquids on the shelves. He mixed and looked, added more, took some out, then he was finally ready. He placed the cup in the wooden bowl full of an exotic blend of several ingredients.

"If this turns bright golden yellow, it is the real cup, if it disintegrates then it is not the cup." Merlin walked back over to us. "Who is chasing you? Can you tell me what is happening?"

"Yes, it's a good story." Casey continued. When she finished, Merlin stood up.

"Let me check on the cup, that is a great story and it isn't over yet. We need to make sure the four of you get home safely from our time." He walked over and looked inside the bowl.

"It did not disintegrate! It is real! This is so amazing! Where is Lamorak?" Merlin took the cup out, dried it and looked at the door of his house.

Lamorak and King Arthur walked through right at that moment.

"It's the real thing!" He handed the cup to Arthur. He looked at it and was amazed. Then he looked up and greeted everyone. Sophia introduced Casey again, Peter and the dogs.

"What can we do for you to repay you for this find?" King Arthur asked.

"King Arthur," Sophia asked, "there are bad men that followed them through trying to steal that cup and trying to kill them. Can anything be done?"

"Yes, Lamorak, call a meeting of the Round Table, we will meet right away. Let everyone know the quest is off for now. I'll be right over as soon as I finish here." King Arthur directed Lamorak.

"Yes Sir, it was nice meeting all of you. I'll try to catch you before you leave." Then Lamorak left.

"This is just amazing." King Arthur smiled, "We would have never found it if as you say the Knights Templar found it first. Now it will go down in history that Camelot holds the Holy Grail. We must make a special case for it and have it secure but displayed by the altar in the church."

"Yes, that is a good idea. I'll look into that right as soon as I can, where do you want to secure it now?" Merlin asked.

"Can you lock it in the vault for safe keeping tonight?" King Arthur asked.

"Will it be secure there?" Peter asked. "I'm only asking because these men will stop at nothing to steal it."

"Hm, Merlin, perhaps it is safer hidden with you?" King Arthur asked.

"Yes, I believe it is. They would never think of robbing me and couldn't get in here. They would break into a vault." Merlin took the cup from Arthur and looked around. He walked over behind his work bench and opened a cover on the floor. He grabbed a cloth and put it in the hole, placing the cover back into place, then moved a table over it.

"There, what do you think?" Merlin asked.

"That should do it." Peter said.

"Yes, I think until this situation is concluded that is a good place. Well, I must go back to the castle. I will see all of you before you leave.

Thank you for finding this and bringing it here." Then King Arthur left.

Merlin looked at us, "Can I get you any tea?"

"No, thank you Merlin, I think we will go back to our place. My friends are tired and hungry. We'll catch you later." Sophia laughed. "You didn't say anything, Merlin when I said that. I think you're getting used me."

Merlin laughed, "Yes, I am getting used to your idiosyncratic use of our language. There are times I am not certain we are speaking the same language. Your form of English has some rather odd word uses. I will talk to you later."

Casey and Peter thanked Merlin, and then we left to go to Sophia's.

It was amazing to be here again in my lifetime. Who would have ever guessed that we would time travel? I felt good that we could get back even if Casey's necklace wouldn't work. I remembered how we got here and back last time. I better check with Kanani that the opening is still active. We had dinner and then all of us went on a walk through the village. Sophia took us to her sister's house for a visit, then we walked through a garden. Casey was tired, and Sophia noticed, so we returned to her house to get a good night's sleep. We had dragons protecting us and a soft bed. What more could a German Shepherd want?

Maybe the bad guys to go away forever!!!!

Not happening! That night we heard shouting and gunfire! Guns have yet to be invented so we knew the bad guys had arrived. Then a scream and silence. I jumped out of bed and barked. Peter opened the bedroom door, Casey was right behind him and T.J. was by me. Sophia came out of her room.

"Did you hear that gunshot? We don't have guns in this time period. I hope everyone is ok! Do we dare open the door?" Sophia asked.

Peter answered her question by opening the front door. I ran out with him, just in time to see Gunther breathing fire down on some men!

Peter jumped back, "Wow, stay inside Ladies! It isn't safe out here."

Lamorak came running over, "Is everyone alright? I heard a strange loud noise. Where's Sophia?"

"She's in the house, I made them go back inside." Peter told him.

"Good, one of the guys got away, Gunther fried this one. We caught them breaking into the castle and chased them out. They shot fire at us with a weapon! This is unheard of. Thank goodness for the dragons, those men would have beat us! Unbelievable! I'm going to check on Sophia right now." Lamorak put his sword in his belt and walked quickly past Peter into the house.

Peter, T.J. and I followed him. He knocked on the door and Sophia opened it. He took her into his arms.

"I was worried about you, my Lady."

"I am fine, thank you Lamorak." Sophia hugged him.

"Good, Casey you are very fortunate that Gunther got one of the men, however one got away. We need to hunt him down. I want all of you to lock up and stay inside. I will be back when we catch him." Lamorak let go of Sophia.

"Lamorak, I'm going with you to find this guy." Peter insisted.

"No, it is too dangerous." Lamorak protested.

"I know what he looks like." Peter replied.

"You do have a point, we don't know what he looks like. Ok, but you must stay by my side, I will get you a sword. Can you use one?" Lamorak asked.

"Actually, yes I can. I have taken fencing classes when I was younger. I believe it will come back to me." Peter turned to leave with Lamorak.

"Good." Lamorak opened the door.

"Hold on a minute Peter!" Casey ran over to him. "Be careful, I don't know what I would do without you."

"I will Honey, stay here. I'll be back soon." Peter kissed her and followed Lamorak outside.

"I'm too wound up to sleep Casey, let me make us some tea and we can chat for a bit." Sophia went over and put some water in a pot and placed it on a hanger suspended in the fireplace.

"Sounds good, I will be so glad when this is over. OH NO!" Casey slapped her forehead.

"What is it?" Sophia turned around and looked at her.

"I left my 90-year-old Aunt back in Brazil in a house we bought. She must be worried sick that we haven't returned!"

"On no, I see why you're worried. Well this will be over soon and then you can go home." Sophia brought two cups of mint tea over and place one in front of Casey.

"Thank you. How are you doing Sophia? What has life been like here?" Casey was curious and so was I.

"It's been a dream, I go back once in a while to check on the house and see if John ever returned." Sophia took a sip of tea.

"The military thinks he is gone for good, Sophia, are you going to wait for him forever?" Casey asked.

"No, after seeing how you married such a wonderful man, I can't let Lamorak slip through my fingers. I have just now made up my mind. I will tell him I have decided to marry him." Sophia smiled.

"Wonderful Sophia! You must let me know and perhaps we can come back." Casey frowned. "Is that opening you came through still working?"

"Oh that! Yes, it is. The Knight Templars have made a border out of it. Anyone wanting to leave, needs a letter from King Arthur, anyone coming in has to have a letter of good character. Then they can only stay for a week unless they have a special permit to stay. This was done after too many of our people wandered into the future and didn't come back. Plus, we don't want any modern terrorists to come here into our time. We have enough trouble with sorcery, druids, and witchcraft. It's all that Arthur can do to keep it out of Camelot. Casey, do you think it's wrong for me to marry Lamorak and change the future of his life?" Sophia asked.

"That's a hard question for me to answer, Sophia. You need to listen to your soul and do what is right. You know he dies young at the hand of another king's son, a King whom Lamorak killed years ago." Casey replied.

"Yes, I know. He killed the King in self-defense for the safety of Camelot, I have to prevent his early death if I can. I have also made sure that Lancelot doesn't bewitch Guinevere. Arthur will have a different ending as well. Then there is Mordred, my sister and I have made sure he stays away. Merlin has helped us with that and he has kept Morgana away from Camelot too. I know it sounds like this is just a perfect world we are making, but it's our life now in this world. I know that King Arthur was not a myth and the history books will be different in the future from what we learned growing up."

Sophia took another sip of tea. "It's very fascinating, do you know that I trust the future will not be drastically or deleteriously changed. I have a house down the road in 2017? I can show you tomorrow exactly where it is. How funny, I have thought about you ever since I moved into the house. I told Peter about you. I'm glad he finally got to meet you." Casey finished her tea and stood up. "Well, I need to go lie down and try to get a bit of rest. Tomorrow is going to be a big day and we need to get back to our future.

There is no telling what we will find when we return. I believe we will return where we left, under tombs in a cathedral. I hope it isn't sealed up where we can't get out and I hope no bad men are waiting for us there. I guess we've given it enough time and the two that followed us won't be any more trouble after tonight either. Tomorrow, Peter and I will tell you our trouble with these guys and what we have been through. It's quite a story in itself. I feel exhausted and on dire need of some sleep." Casey got up. "Thank you for the tea, Sophia."

"I can't wait to hear your entire story tomorrow, I'm going to wait up a bit, but I'll see you in the morning." Sophia got up to make more tea, as Casey, T.J. and I left the room.

Morning came too early, the sun was shining through the room, so I started licking Casey. I looked around, no Peter. I hoped that he would have been back already.
Sophia knocked on the bedroom door.

Casey got out of bed, "Come in Sophia."

"Good morning, there is still no news and I'm a bit concerned. I thought that we could have a quick breakfast and go to Camelot and see if we find anything out." Sophia smiled.

"I'll be right out, I agree that's a great plan." Casey grabbed her clothes, Sophia left and shut the door.

We had a very silent breakfast. As no one seemed to have much of an appetite. I knew the girls were worried.

We started to walk out the door and then Lamorak came running up to us. "Good, I see you're dressed. I have some stressful news. We must go see Merlin." He looked worriedly at Casey.

"Why? What happened?" Casey begged him.

"We apprehended the man, but he fired a shot and it wounded Peter. He is with Merlin right now getting bandaged up." Lamorak turned to go.

"Oh no! Will he be ok?" Casey cried.
Sophia put her arm around Casey.

"We hope so, he has lost a bit of blood, but Merlin is hopeful. Come, let's hurry." Lamorak put his hand on Sophia's back.

Casey was holding back tears, I rubbed up against her and she put her hand on my head. "Thank you, Jackie Lee."

I just wagged my tail, I wanted this not to be happening any more than Casey. T.J. had his tail down and he was crying. Casey bent down and hugged him.

We got to Merlin's door and Lamorak opened it up for us to go inside.

"Casey," Merlin said, "Come here and let me tell you what has happened."

Casey walked over and sat in the chair by the bed.

"Peter has lost some blood, he is very week. I have given him a sedative to rest. There is a spell I can do and it will heal him, but there must be no talk of this outside this room. He looked around. Does everyone agree?"

"Yes, everyone replied."

"Good, Arthur lets me do magic for good, but he frowns upon it as too many have used their magic for evil. I will make a potion and work on him. Please give me a moment." Merlin left and went back to his work bench. It was about half an hour later when he came back.

"Here, Casey help me give this to him." Merlin gave Casey the Holy Grail. "I'm going to say some words, he will wake and you must have him drink this right away."

Casey shook her head in agreement.

Peter heard Casey and opened his eyes, then tried to smile.

"You must drink this, Honey." Casey leaned over Peter and helped him drink the potion. Peter sank back on the bed. We looked and the wound began to close, it took about 10 minutes and Peter didn't have a scratch on him! We couldn't even do that in modern times. I wonder how this art was lost? I hoped that Casey would ask Merlin, because I wanted to know. It wasn't long before Peter was able to sit up.

"Merlin, I can't thank you enough." Peter told him.

Casey was crying tears of joy. "Thank you, Merlin."

"You are very welcome, I'm glad it worked. Now, the man that did that is sentenced to death. He will hang tomorrow. There won't be any more threats coming from the two men that followed you from the future." Merlin smiled.

Casey stood up, "We really can't thank you enough."

"You have thanked all of us, you brought us the Holy Grail. Without that Grail, my medicine and words would not have worked." Merlin finished saying.

That's how it worked! I got my answer, I wagged my tail.

Peter felt good enough to leave, so we left Merlin and then ran into King Arthur, we thank him and said our goodbyes. Sophia called on Emmorous to take us back where he found us. Casey wasn't sure that mattered, but we didn't want to chance not going back home in the corrected time period.

We said our goodbyes to everyone, I was going to miss Kanani. Sophia had tears in her eyes as we took off on Emmorous. Casey and Peter waved, it was sad that we may never see them in our lifetime again. Emmorous dropped us off and watched us disappear.

We landed in the same place we disappeared from.

"Is everyone in one piece?" Peter asked.

Casey laughed, "Yes, we made it back!" She hugged him and looked around. Look Honey, they have begun excavating the treasure, the opening above is opened and I hear people."

"Let's go check it out. Follow me." Peter started up the stairs and all of us followed.

"Well, hi there. You must be the people that found this treasure. We were wondering what happened to you." The parish priest came over and shook Peter's hand. He had a cast on his left arm. "Those thugs disappeared, so we didn't know if you were ok or not."

"It is us, we found a time machine and vanished. They found one too, because they followed us. One died by dragon fire, the other one is being hung today. What about the rest of the gang?" Peter asked.

"Mr. Schim has been here with men, they rounded up the ones they could get." The priest answered.

"We have to get back to Casey's aunt." Peter told him.

"Aunt Claire and Chela are just fine. Chela's family has been freed. This is a great find, it's all going into a museum." The priest assured us.

"Fantastic, well, we must go home. We are happy you are ok." Casey told the priest.

"Blessings, have a splendid day." The priest nodded that he too was happy he was ok, then he waved at us as we left.

Our car was still parked where we left it. 4 hours later we arrived at our place. There were two cars there. As we parked and got out Baron walked outside with another man, that must be Mr. Schim.

"Baron! You flew all the way here to help Aunt Claire! Thank you." Casey ran into his arms.

"Ha, of course I did. Scott is holding down the fort at home. I couldn't wait to help out."

Baron shook Peter's hand. "Look, Mr. Schim came by too."

"Good to meet you Mr. Schim," Casey shook his hand as did Peter.

"It's great meeting you as well. The danger you put yourself in has paid off very well. This is a treasure like no other." He said shaking his head.

If only he knew about the Holy Grail. I said to T.J.

T.J. nodded his head. He agreed with me.

Aunt Claire was so happy to see us, she cried. Chela was gone, she had gone home to her family. We stayed a few more days then flew home to England. When we got to our house, Scott and Captain were waiting. It was a joyous reunion. We had achieved what we were looking for; one of the treasures stolen by the Nazi's from the Knights Templars and buried in Brazil. Would we ever go back to Camelot? I bet we would, we've been there twice now. OH, get a load of this! Casey is calling us all together.

"I want to thank everyone for helping with this crusade, I was hoping for some time off, but look at this email I just received!

Dear Ms. Casey Lane,

I am in need of finding a carousel horse that has treasure or a map in it. My grandfather owned it and I found a copy of a letter he had hidden in the nook of his old desk. I hoped that you would consider taking on my hunt. I heard that you are very good at solving crimes and finding treasures. I also heard that you had a grandfather that collected carousel horses. Perhaps you could call me as soon as possible.

It was signed Sir John Luis, his address and phone number.

Peter looked at Casey. "Well?" Peter asked.

"I don't know, it sounds intriguing." Casey looked at Baron, "What do you think?"

Baron laughed, "Why not?"

Scott chimed in, "I'm in too and I know that Robert and Jack will be only too happy to help."

"Speaking of them, where are they?" Casey asked.

"They went to pick up some dinner for all of us and should be here soon." Scott said.

"Ok, then I guess I'll answer this Sir person and see what happens. We need to look at those horses in the basement again, go over them more carefully." Casey had that look in her eyes.

Just then the door opened, Robert and Jack walked in with Pizza and wine. There were hugs all around, they would be delighted to help. Jack had made a full recovery.

It was just like nothing had happened, we had Captain with us, we promised to never leave him again.

That night I dreamed about a carousel horse.............

THE END

Read on to get a taste of another

Exciting adventure

By J.M.M. ADAMS

SOPHIA

and

the

DRAGON

1

"SOPHIE!" Susan screams as Sophia disappears into the opening of the cave.

"Kanani no! Come back!" Leila called too late. Susan and Leila watch Kanani vanish through the portal.

Sophia tumbled through darkness for a long moment, then landed awkwardly and tumbled to the ground. She didn't know what had happened to her, so she looked around. She was on the ground beside a dirt road; across the road to her right was what looked like an English Pub. There was a bit of haze with the sun shining through and the air was humid, she could feel her hair starting to frizz around her face.

She thought to herself; *did I just go through time? This is unbelievable. I thought I could do that in Egypt?*

She struggled to her feet only to be knocked down again when Kanani tumbled from the portal, crashing into the back of her knees.

"Kanani, I'm glad to see you too and that you love me so much. I love you even more! Now can you please stop jumping back and forth over me?" She begged her German Shepherd as she struggled to stand back up.

I love you too Sophie, I'm just so happy to see you.

Thought Kanani, as she licked Sophie's face.

Sophia stood up and straightened out her jean skirt, dusting off her black t-shirt.

Look out Sophie! *There's a strange person approaching us.* Kanani was barking warning Sophia.

Sophia heard a horse and looked up. Someone tall rode a big, black stallion towards them. As the rider drew near, Sophia caught the pale glint of sunlight off chain armor. He stopped in front of them and dismounted. He looked in his late twenties, about Sophia's age. He took his helmet off and tucked it under his arm. His long sandy blond hair fell out from under it. He was about six feet tall with a muscular build and the most beautiful blue eyes She had ever seen.

"Stop barking Kanani," Sophia scolded her German Shepherd.

Kanani stopped barking, *Ok, Sophie, but he better not hurt us.*

"Good day Madam, are you alright?"

"Yes, yes, I think so, thank you for stopping to ask." Sophia stuttered as she continued looking around, still wondering where they were. It looked a lot like Cornwall, but not the Cornwall she was familiar with.

"Who are you?"

"I'm Sophia and this is Kanani, we were exploring caves with my friends and ended up here. May I ask who you are and where I am?"

"Yes, my Lady it is the year of our Lord, 1180, you are in the County of Devon and I am Sir Lamorak de Gales. I am a Knight of the Round Table in King Arthur's court.

"May I pet your animal, Lady?" he asked without waiting for Sophia to answer him. He bent over to pet Kanani. Sophia was so glad Kanani didn't bite him.

"If she lets you pet her it's ok with me," Sophia managed to say.

I guess if he pets me he's ok Sophie. Kanani wagged her tail.

"I've never seen a dog like this and I have never seen anyone dressed like you." Said sir Lamorak.

Yeah, we've never seen anyone dressed like you either buddy, Kanani was saying with her tongue hanging out of her mouth.

Sophia's heart was beating so fast she was sure he could hear it.

Here I was dressed like a person from my time, at least I had leggings under my shirt. My hair probably didn't look bad, it was long, dark blonde and braided. Was

I really standing here talking to a handsome knight? Sophia thought to herself.

"My dog is an Alsatian," Sophia hoped that would be less confusing than German Shepherd.

"Where are you from?" He asked studying her more closely.

"I'm from Luxembourg. But I'm from the year of our Lord 2013," She whispered.

"Did you say 2013? Did you come here on purpose? I don't understand how that happened." He looked amazed.

"No, it was an accident. I'm lost and really want to go back now!" She was unsure of herself and looked back at the rock she and Kanani apparently came through. The portal was not visible to her now though.

He followed her gaze and apparently saw nothing but a rock either.

Kanani looked too and walked over to the rock sniffing. Yeah, I can't believe we came through that either. Sophie sure does some fun things.

"I do not know how to get you back." He took note of dusk starting to fall. You must come to my Castle, I am not going to let a beautiful young lady and dog stand here all night for thieves to rob and kill."

"Your Castle? I don't have anything proper to put

on for a castle visit," She looked down her skirt again, at least she wasn't in shorts!

"I'm sure my mother can find something for you to wear." He said then bent over and gently took her hand, giving it a kiss. Wow, I'll follow you anywhere. Sophia was thinking with a lump in her throat. She was still wondering how she would get back home. She felt a bit of dread in the pit of her stomach as he led her towards his castle.

"Will you remember where you found us?" She asked a bit pleadingly.

"Yes, I will." He turned to look at Sophia, "It's almost dark, and we must hurry."

Sophia grabbed her pack and took Kanani's leash out snapping it on her collar. He walked leading his horse behind them.

Would Susan and Leila get Kimo and come find us? Oh, I shouldn't have listened to Leila and I should have stayed home working on Grandpa's notes in my library in Luxembourg.

Sophia was choking back tears. She was having a hard time letting go since John, her husband, had been killed almost a year ago.

"What is that you have on your dog?" He interrupted Sophia's self-pity.

"It's called a leash; I don't think it's invented yet."

"No, it isn't, I have a lot of questions for you. Don't worry. You will be safe in my care, my Lady."

"I hope so," Sophia answered down cast.

We'll be ok Sophie, he's ok and I'm here with you. Kanani was walking close to Sophie and looking up at her.

As they advanced down the road Sophia looked around, the countryside was green with rolling hills. She decided to try and enjoy her predicament, since she was on this adventure whether She wanted to be or not.

I don't have anything to worry about. Susan and Kimo will take care of Leila and the house in Luxembourg. It is so beautiful here and looks very different from how I remembered it when Jennie and I came here on summer vacations with our Grandma and Grandpa. The farms and roads weren't here now, it was untouched. Being summer, the weather was nice and Kanani didn't seem upset by our recent experience. So, I might as well enjoy my adventure. It would be something else to write about when I got home. Sophia was telling herself.

After walking for about an hour Lamorak pointed at a castle and said with pride in his voice. "There's my castle."

"Wow, it's gorgeous!" Sophia was getting excited forgetting her predicament. She was a bit anxious to meet his family though.

"She has been in my family many years. When my father was slain in battle it became mine, which was five years ago. I now take care of my mother, Lady Yglais." He looked thoughtful.

"I don't think it's a good idea for anyone to know where you have come from, at least not today. My mother will wonder if she sees the way you are dressed. I will put you into a spare bedchamber right away, and then go find her. I will mention I met you, but not tell Her where you came from."

He was still talking, but he lost Sophia's attention, because they had just entered the most magnificent castle she had ever seen! They were walking through the courtyard no one was about.

She followed him into the stables. He handed his horse over to a page. The page looked at Sophia with suspicion, but didn't say anything.

"Oh, he gives me the chills, he is staring at me Sir Lamorak."

"Never mind him. Come let's get you and your dog

into the castle."

He pushed her gently in front of him to leave the stable. Then Kanani and Sophia followed Lamorak into the main hall of the castle. She tried looking around at everything without tripping, but had a hard time, because He was moving her rapidly to their room. They got there and He opened up the doors.

"This will be your chamber, please go in quickly." Lamorak told her.

She looked around at the beautiful room; there was a bed, washstand and a window looking out over the moors.

Yahoo, this is a neat pad Sophie. Check out that bed! Kanani bounded into to the room jumping on the bed, and then jumped off.

"Well your dog likes the room," laughed Lamorak.

"Make yourself comfortable and I will have some dresses and clothing brought in for you, my Lady. Don't be frightened, are you?"

"Not so much frightened, as concerned if I will be accepted. Then there's that little thing about how long I'll be here." She pinched herself, *yep, she was awake, and this was not a dream.* He saw her pinching herself.

"I don't understand how you got here, but

everything will work out. I am pleased that I was the one that found you. This will put some excitement into our lives," he said with a bid of glee in his voice, and then he grinned turning around to walk out the door. He stopped remembering something, turned back to her around said; "I will escort you to dinner in two hours."

"Great, thank you."

Then he closed the door and disappeared.

"Doesn't he suspect I were going to try and get back home?" She said to Kanani as she took off her backpack and looked inside to see what Susan had loaded into it that morning.

No, I don't think so Sophie, but don't worry this is fun. Kanani looked in the bag with Sophia. She found the phone Grandpa had given her for the planned time travel in Egypt.

She had planned on going back in time to try to find her sister and brother -in -law. Jennie had disappeared over a year ago while on an excavation trip with her husband and Leila. Leila had stayed behind in the camp that morning. They never returned to her. That's how Leila had come to live in Luxembourg under Sophia's care. Grandpa had told her this phone worked for time travel; well she was going to give it a test after getting cleaned up. She felt and looked grubby and dirty. She walked over to the basin of water and washed her face, then looked into the mirror sighing. Of course, she had no makeup in her pack. She was going to miss a lot of things. A knock at the door startled her.

"Come in."

The door opened and a young maid walked in carrying ten gowns, then another one followed her carrying more clothes. They were gorgeous gowns; Sophia couldn't believe it!

"Look at those dresses! I am so thankful; I don't know what to say except thank you."

"You're very welcome Lady," said the first maid. "I will hang them up in the closet; do you need anything else or help with anything my Lady?"

"Yes, I need to know what to wear to dinner tonight, and I need some face stuff to make me pretty."

"Afawen," she pointed to the other girl, "put some makeup over there for you by the basin, if you need other colors let me know. There is also some lotion with it, would you like some hot water to be brought in for a bath?"

"I would love that so much!" Exclaimed Sophia.

"Ok, my name is Bryn and we will be back soon," but instead of leaving she walked over to the hanging gowns and pulled one out. "This blue one would look very nice on you tonight." She said holding it up for inspection.

It was the most gorgeous blue gown Sophia had ever seen. "Thank you. That one will do fine. It's nice to meet you Bryn. My name is Sophia; my friends call me Sophie."

"Your welcome, I will be here to assist you for your stay. Then she giggled, looking down at Kanani. May I pet her? She's so pretty."

"Yes, let me introduce you to Kanani." Sophia walked over and knelt down by her dog, then invited Bryn to come over and pet her.

"Thank you, my Lady," then she stood up. "I'll be back with your hot water very soon." She turned and walked out of the room.

"What an endearing young lady." Sophia said to Kanani and then sighed, "This might be fun, I'm going to try and call Grandpa."

Kanani was looking around the room and thinking, *Not bad for a place to stay. I wonder where we are? Yes, Sophie, this will be fun, Woof woof!*

Sophia knew that Susan and Leila were probably frantic that she and Kanani had disappeared.

Picking up the phone She dialed the number

Grandpa had given her. It rang only once to her great relief. She heard his voice on the other end of it.

"Hello. Sophie is this you my dear?"

"Hi Grandpa. Yes, it's me and I want you to know that I am ok and it's so nice to hear your voice!"

"It's nice to hear your voice too, my dear. Susan and Kimo called telling me about your disappearance right after it happened. They were very upset, but I calmed them down. We'll figure out how to get you home. What year did you land in sweetheart?"

"I landed in 1180 and I'm staying at Sir Lamorak de Gales castle in Devon, England. He is a knight in King Arthur's court, can you Google Him Grandpa, and let me know whatever you can find out about him?" She pleaded.

"Yes, dear I can do that for you. Are they treating you like the princess you are to me?" The warmth in his voice quieted her.

"Yes, Grandpa they are; I have ten beautiful gowns hanging in my wardrobe! Lamorak acts like I'm here to stay forever!"

"Well, sweetheart this is good for you to have a little adventure. I want you to start living again after your heartache of losing John," he told her endearingly.

"I know Grandpa, but this is strange, oh, someone is

knocking on my door; I'll call you back tomorrow. Please let everyone know I'm ok. I love you Grandpa."

"Ok, sweetheart I will and I love you too," then he hung up.

Sophia tossed the phone in her pack and hurried over to open the door. The castle attendants were carrying her bath water, soap and anything else she needed. They filled the tub and as they were leaving Bryn walked in.

"Well it looks in place, my Lady. Can I be of help with your bath or help you dress?"

"Yes, could you come back in thirty minutes and help me with the dress? I would be grateful."

"Yes, I can, now enjoy your hot bath my Lady and I will be back soon." Bryn left closing the door behind her.

"I will," shouted Sophia after her.

It looked like a lovely bath, Sophia peeled off her dirty clothes, folding them and placing them in her pack. Then she stepped into the hot inviting bath. It felt good on her aching muscles and she relaxed. Not having much time, because Bryn would be back soon, she got out and dried off. She was just slipping the dress on when there was a knock on the door.

"Bryn, is that you?"

"Yes, my lady. May I come in now?" She asked.

"Yes, I'm ready for you."

She entered and asked, "How was your bath?"

"Fantastic! It picked up my spirit and I needed that."

"Good," she helped button up the dress and apply face color. When they were all done Bryn looked at her.

"You look lovely, my Lady. Yes, you will do."

"Really? Thank you so much!" Sophia gave Bryn a hug, which made her blush.

"I will make sure Kanani is fed, what does she eat?" Bryn asked.

Well, as long as she feeds me what I like, come on Sophie, tell her what I like to eat. Kanani was thumping her tail at Bryn.

"She can eat meat and needs drinking water. I would really appreciate that, thank you." Sophia said.

"Your welcome, I'll be back after you go to dinner and take care of her."

"Thank you again Bryn," then she left. Sophia hugged Kanani; she just cocked her and gave Sophia a look.

"We're going to be ok, sweetie. Bryn will come back with your food and take you out for potty. I love you Nani!" Sophia buried her face into Kanani's neck.

I love you too, don't be gone too long. Kanani didn't want her to leave at all.

Then there was a knock on the door, letting go of Kanani Sophia walked over and opened it up. Handsome Sir Lamorak was standing there!

"Good evening," Sophia said, "do you like how I look now?" She asked him twirling around.

Then she really looked at him, he was so handsome in his blue linen shirt and black pants. The blue shirt brought out the blue of his eyes. Oh, she could fall for him.

"You are very beautiful my Lady," he replied, "I am honored to escort you to dinner." Then he stuck out his arm for Sophia to take hold of. She looked back at Kanani and told her to be a good girl. That she would be back soon. Sophia was really nervous.

They walked into the dining room. Everyone was already seated.

"Mother, I would like to introduce you to Lady Sophia of Luxembourg," Lamorak stepped back to show off Sophia and introduce her to his mother. She was shocked he called her that, how was she going to pull this one off?

"Very nice to meet you Lady Yglais," she said with a curtsy.

"It's very nice to meet you as well, let me introduce you to everyone, my dear." Lady Yglais continued. She pointed as she spoke, "The man to my left is my other son, Perceval; next to him is Accalon and then his wife Cundrie. Accalon is my nephew and both he and his wife are staying here with us for the time being. Why don't you sit here next to me on my right, dear?" She patted the seat next to her.

"Hello, it's nice to meet all of you," Sophia said, then turned to Yglais, Lamorak's mother, "I am honored to sit next to you my Lady, thank you."

Lamorak pulled out the chair and she sat down. Sophia made it through dinner without any mishaps. Stories were told about the quests the knights had been on. Then she heard about how King Arthur had called everyone into his Kingdom for a festival starting tomorrow. Cundrie talked about what clothes to pack, Lady Yglais said that everyone should get up early, because the wagons needed to be packed up. Lady Yglais told Sophia that she was invited to go with them. Then the conversation changed and she asked Sophia if she loved children. Sophia told her yes, that she wanted to open a school someday. Lady Yglais thought that was a great idea. Sophia didn't mean for her to think she was opening one here! They talked about that for a while. After dinner was over the Page, Iago came in and gestured for Cundrie to leave and talk to him. Sophia wondered what that was about. No one else seemed to bother about it, so Sophia let it go.

Lamorak and his mother walked Sophia back to her room talking about what she needed to take for the trip to Camelot.

Sophia was a bit anxious how Kanani had done without her. She opened the door to her room, turned to say goodnight and thanked both of them for the lovely evening.

"I'll see you early in the morning, goodnight kind sir."

"Good night Lady Yglais, thank you for your hospitality."

"Good night my Lady," Lamorak and his mother both said, then they turned to walk away.

Sophia closed the door and screamed!!!!

"SOPHIE!" Susan screams as Sophia disappears into the opening of the cave.

"Kanani no! Come back!" Leila called too late. Susan and Leila watch Kanani vanish through the portal.

Sophia tumbled through darkness for a

long moment, then landed awkwardly and tumbled to the ground. She didn't know what had happened to her, so she looked around. She was on the ground beside a dirt road; across the road to her right was what looked like an English Pub. There was a bit of haze with the sun shining through and the air was humid, she could feel her hair starting to frizz around her face.

She thought to herself; did I just go through time? This is unbelievable. I thought I could do that in Egypt?

She struggled to her feet only to be knocked down again when Kanani tumbled from the portal, crashing into the back of her knees.

"Kanani, I'm glad to see you too and that you love me so much. I love you even more! Now can you please stop jumping back and forth over me?" She begged her German Shepherd as she struggled to stand back up.

I love you too Sophie, I'm just so happy to see you. Thought Kanani, as she licked Sophie's face.

Sophia stood up and straightened out her

jean skirt, dusting off her black t-shirt.

Look out Sophie! There's a strange person approaching us. Kanani was barking warning Sophia.

Sophia heard a horse and looked up. Someone tall rode a big, black stallion towards them. As the rider drew near, Sophia caught the pale glint of sunlight off chain armor. He stopped in front of them and dismounted. He looked in his late twenties, about Sophia's age. He took his helmet off and tucked it under his arm. His long sandy blond hair fell out from under it. He was about six feet tall with a muscular build and the most beautiful blue eyes She had ever seen.

"Stop barking Kanani," Sophia scolded her German Shepherd.

Kanani stopped barking, Ok, Sophie, but he better not hurt us.

"Good day Madam, are you alright?"

"Yes, yes, I think so, thank you for stopping to ask." Sophia stuttered as she continued looking around, still wondering where they were. It looked a lot like Cornwall, but not the Cornwall she was familiar with.

"Who are you?"

"I'm Sophia and this is Kanani, we were exploring caves with my friends and ended up here. May I ask who you are and where I am?"

"Yes, my Lady it is the year of our Lord, 1180, you are in the County of Devon and I am Sir Lamorak de Gales. I am a Knight of the Round Table in King Arthur's court.

"May I pet your animal, Lady?" he asked without waiting for Sophia to answer him. He bent over to pet Kanani. Sophia was so glad Kanani didn't bite him.

"If she lets you pet her it's ok with me," Sophia managed to say.

I guess if he pets me he's ok Sophie. Kanani wagged her tail.

"I've never seen a dog like this and I have never seen anyone dressed like you." Said sir Lamorak.

Yeah, we've never seen anyone dressed like you either buddy, Kanani was saying with her tongue hanging out of her mouth.

Sophia's heart was beating so fast she was sure he could hear it.

Here I was dressed like a person from my time, at least I had leggings under my shirt. My hair probably didn't look bad, it was long, dark blonde and braided. Was I really standing here talking to a handsome knight? Sophia thought to herself.

"My dog is an Alsatian," Sophia hoped that would be less confusing than German Shepherd.

"Where are you from?" He asked studying her more closely.

"I'm from Luxembourg. But I'm from the year of our Lord 2013," She whispered.

"Did you say 2013? Did you come here on purpose? I don't understand how that happened." He looked amazed.

"No, it was an accident. I'm lost and really want to go back now!" She was unsure of herself and looked back at the rock she and Kanani apparently came through. The portal was not visible to her now though.

He followed her gaze and apparently saw nothing but a rock either.

Kanani looked too and walked over to the rock sniffing. Yeah, I can't believe we came through that either. Sophie sure does some fun things.

"I do not know how to get you back." He took note of dusk starting to fall. You must come to my Castle, I am not going to let a beautiful young lady and dog stand here all night for thieves to rob and kill."

"Your Castle? I don't have anything proper to put on for a castle visit," She looked down her skirt again, at least she wasn't in shorts!

"I'm sure my mother can find something for you to wear." He said then bent over and gently took her hand, giving it a kiss. Wow, I'll follow you anywhere. Sophia was thinking with a lump in her throat. She was still wondering how she would get back home. She felt a bit of dread in the pit of her stomach as he led her towards his castle.

"Will you remember where you found us?" She asked a bit pleadingly.

"Yes, I will." He turned to look at Sophia,

"It's almost dark, and we must hurry."

Sophia grabbed her pack and took Kanani's leash out snapping it on her collar. He walked leading his horse behind them.

Would Susan and Leila get Kimo and come find us? Oh, I shouldn't have listened to Leila and I should have stayed home working on Grandpa's notes in my library in Luxembourg.

Sophia was choking back tears. She was having a hard time letting go since John, her husband, had been killed almost a year ago.

"What is that you have on your dog?" He interrupted Sophia's self-pity.

"It's called a leash; I don't think it's invented yet."

"No, it isn't, I have a lot of questions for you. Don't worry. You will be safe in my care, my Lady."

"I hope so," Sophia answered down cast.

We'll be ok Sophie, he's ok and I'm here with you. Kanani was walking close to Sophie and looking up at her.

As they advanced down the road Sophia looked around, the countryside was green with rolling hills. She decided to try and enjoy her predicament, since she was on this adventure whether She wanted to be or not.

I don't have anything to worry about. Susan and Kimo will take care of Leila and the house in Luxembourg. It is so beautiful here and looks very different from how I remembered it when Jennie and I came here on summer vacations with our Grandma and Grandpa. The farms and roads weren't here now, it was untouched. Being summer, the weather was nice and Kanani didn't seem upset by our recent experience. So, I might as well enjoy my adventure. It would be something else to write about when I got home. Sophia was telling herself.

After walking for about an hour Lamorak pointed at a castle and said with pride in his voice. "There's my castle."

"Wow, it's gorgeous!" Sophia was getting excited forgetting her predicament. She was a bit anxious to meet his family though.

"She has been in my family many years. When my father was slain in battle it became mine, which was five years ago. I now take care of my mother, Lady Yglais." He looked thoughtful.

"I don't think it's a good idea for anyone to know where you have come from, at least not today. My mother will wonder if she sees the way you are dressed. I will put you into a spare bedchamber right away, and then go find her. I will mention I met you, but not tell Her where you came from."

He was still talking, but he lost Sophia's attention, because they had just entered the most magnificent castle she had ever seen! They were walking through the courtyard no one was about.

She followed him into the stables. He handed his horse over to a page. The page looked at Sophia with suspicion, but didn't say anything.

"Oh, he gives me the chills, he is staring at me Sir Lamorak."

"Never mind him. Come let's get you and your dog into the castle."

He pushed her gently in front of him to

leave the stable. Then Kanani and Sophia followed Lamorak into the main hall of the castle. She tried looking around at everything without tripping, but had a hard time, because He was moving her rapidly to their room. They got there and He opened up the doors.

"This will be your chamber, please go in quickly." Lamorak told her.

She looked around at the beautiful room; there was a bed, washstand and a window looking out over the moors.

Yahoo, this is a neat pad Sophie. Check out that bed! Kanani bounded into to the room jumping on the bed, and then jumped off.

"Well your dog likes the room," laughed Lamorak.

"Make yourself comfortable and I will have some dresses and clothing brought in for you, my Lady. Don't be frightened, are you?"

"Not so much frightened, as concerned if I will be accepted. Then there's that little thing about how long I'll be here." She pinched herself, yep, she was awake, and this was not a dream. He saw her pinching herself.

"I don't understand how you got here, but everything will work out. I am pleased that I was the one that found you. This will put some excitement into our lives," he said with a bid of glee in his voice, and then he grinned turning around to walk out the door. He stopped remembering something, turned back to her around said; "I will escort you to dinner in two hours."

"Great, thank you."

Then he closed the door and disappeared.

"Doesn't he suspect I were going to try and get back home?" She said to Kanani as she took off her backpack and looked inside to see what Susan had loaded into it that morning.

No I don't think so Sophie, but don't worry this is fun. Kanani looked in the bag with Sophia. She found the phone Grandpa had given her for the planned time travel in Egypt.

She had planned on going back in time to try to find her sister and brother -in -law. Jennie had disappeared over a year ago while on an excavation trip with her husband and Leila.

Leila had stayed behind in the camp that morning. They never returned to her. That's how Leila had come to live in Luxembourg under Sophia's care. Grandpa had told her this phone worked for time travel; well she was going to give it a test after getting cleaned up. She felt and looked grubby and dirty. She walked over to the basin of water and washed her face, then looked into the mirror sighing. Of course she had no makeup in her pack. She was going to miss a lot of things. A knock at the door startled her.

"Come in."

The door opened and a young maid walked in carrying ten gowns, then another one followed her carrying more clothes. They were gorgeous gowns; Sophia couldn't believe it!

"Look at those dresses! I am so thankful; I don't know what to say except thank you."

"You're very welcome Lady," said the first maid. "I will hang them up in the closet; do you need anything else or help with anything my Lady?"

"Yes, I need to know what to wear to dinner tonight, and I need some face stuff to make me pretty."

"Afawen," she pointed to the other girl, "put some makeup over there for you by the basin, if you need other colors let me know. There is also some lotion with it, would you like some hot water to be brought in for a bath?"

"I would love that so much!" Exclaimed Sophia.

"Ok, my name is Bryn and we will be back soon," but instead of leaving she walked over to the hanging gowns and pulled one out. "This blue one would look very nice on you tonight." She said holding it up for inspection.

It was the most gorgeous blue gown Sophia had ever seen. "Thank you. That one will do fine. It's nice to meet you Bryn. My name is Sophia; my friends call me Sophie."

"Your welcome, I will be here to assist you for your stay. Then she giggled, looking down at Kanani. May I pet her? She's so pretty."

"Yes, let me introduce you to Kanani." Sophia walked over and knelt down by her dog, then invited Bryn to come over and pet her.

"Thank you my Lady," then she stood up.

"I'll be back with your hot water very soon." She turned and walked out of the room.

"What an endearing young lady." Sophia said to Kanani and then sighed, "This might be fun, I'm going to try and call Grandpa."

Kanani was looking around the room and thinking, Not bad for a place to stay. I wonder where we are? Yes, Sophie, this will be fun, Woof woof!

Sophia knew that Susan and Leila were probably frantic that she and Kanani had disappeared.

Picking up the phone She dialed the number Grandpa had given her. It rang only once to her great relief. She heard his voice on the other end of it.

"Hello. Sophie is this you my dear?"

"Hi Grandpa. Yes, it's me and I want you to know that I am ok and it's so nice to hear your voice!"

"It's nice to hear your voice too, my dear. Susan and Kimo called telling me about your disappearance right after it happened. They were very upset, but I calmed them down. We'll figure out how to get you home. What year did you land in sweetheart?"

"I landed in 1180 and I'm staying at Sir Lamorak de Gales castle in Devon, England. He is a knight in King Arthur's court, can you Google him Grandpa, and let me know whatever you can find out about him?" She pleaded.

"Yes, dear I can do that for you. Are they treating you like the princess you are to me?" The warmth in his voice quieted her.

"Yes, Grandpa they are; I have ten beautiful gowns hanging in my wardrobe! Lamorak acts like I'm here to stay forever!"

"Well, sweetheart this is good for you to have a little adventure. I want you to start living again after your heartache of losing John," he told her endearingly.

"I know Grandpa, but this is strange, oh, someone is knocking on my door; I'll call you back tomorrow. Please let everyone know I'm ok. I love you Grandpa."

"Ok, sweetheart I will and I love you too," then he hung up.

Sophia tossed the phone in her pack and

hurried over to open the door. The castle attendants were carrying her bath water, soap and anything else she needed. They filled the tub and as they were leaving Bryn walked in.

"Well it looks in place, my Lady. Can I be of help with your bath or help you dress?"

"Yes, could you come back in thirty minutes and help me with the dress? I would be grateful."

"Yes I can, now enjoy your hot bath my Lady and I will be back soon." Bryn left closing the door behind her.

"I will," shouted Sophia after her.

It looked like a lovely bath, Sophia peeled off her dirty clothes, folding them and placing them in her pack. Then she stepped into the hot inviting bath. It felt good on her aching muscles and she relaxed. Not having much time, because Bryn would be back soon, she got out and dried off. She was just slipping the dress on when there was a knock on the door.

"Bryn, is that you?"

"Yes, my lady. May I come in now?" She asked.

"Yes, I'm ready for you."

She entered and asked, "How was your bath?"

"Fantastic! It picked up my spirit and I needed that."

"Good," she helped button up the dress and apply face color. When they were all done Bryn looked at her.

"You look lovely, my Lady. Yes, you will do."

"Really? Thank you so much!" Sophia gave Bryn a hug, which made her blush.

"I will make sure Kanani is fed, what does she eat?" Bryn asked.

Well, as long as she feeds me what I like, come on Sophie, tell her what I like to eat. Kanani was thumping her tail at Bryn.

"She can eat meat and needs drinking water. I would really appreciate that, thank you." Sophia said.

"Your welcome, I'll be back after you go to dinner and take care of her."

"Thank you again Bryn," then she left. Sophia hugged Kanani; she just cocked her and gave Sophia a look.

"We're going to be ok, sweetie. Bryn will come back with your food and take you out for potty. I love you Nani!" Sophia buried her face into Kanani's neck.

I love you too, don't be gone too long. Kanani didn't want her to leave at all.

Then there was a knock on the door, letting go of Kanani Sophia walked over and opened it up. Handsome Sir Lamorak was standing there!

"Good evening," Sophia said, "do you like how I look now?" She asked him twirling around.

Then she really looked at him, he was so handsome in his blue linen shirt and black pants. The blue shirt brought out the blue of his eyes. Oh, she could fall for him.

"You are very beautiful my Lady," he replied, "I am honored to escort you to dinner." Then he stuck out his arm for Sophia to take hold of. She looked back at Kanani and told her to be a good girl. That she would be back soon. Sophia was really nervous.

They walked into the dining room. Everyone was already seated.

"Mother, I would like to introduce you to Lady Sophia of Luxembourg," Lamorak stepped back to show off Sophia and introduce her to his mother. She was shocked he called her that, how was she going to pull this one off?

"Very nice to meet you Lady Yglais," she said with a curtsy.

"It's very nice to meet you as well, let me introduce you to everyone, my dear." Lady Yglais continued. She pointed as she spoke, "The man to my left is my other son, Perceval; next to him is Accalon and then his wife Cundrie. Accalon is my nephew and both he and his wife are staying here with us for the time being. Why don't you sit here next to me on my right, dear?" She patted the seat next to her.

"Hello, it's nice to meet all of you," Sophia said, then turned to Yglais, Lamorak's mother, "I am honored to sit next to you my Lady, thank you."

Lamorak pulled out the chair and she sat down. Sophia made it through dinner without any mishaps. Stories were told about the quests the knights had been on. Then she heard about how King Arthur had called everyone into his Kingdom for a festival starting tomorrow. Cundrie talked about what clothes to pack, Lady Yglais said that everyone should get up early, because the wagons needed to be packed up. Lady Yglais told Sophia that she was invited to go with them. Then the conversation changed and she asked Sophia if she loved children. Sophia told her yes, that she wanted to open a school someday. Lady Yglais thought that was a great idea. Sophia didn't mean for her to think she was opening one here! They talked about that for a while. After dinner was over the Page, Iago came in and gestured for Cundrie to leave and talk to him. Sophia wondered what that was about. No one else seemed to bother about it, so Sophia let it go.

Lamorak and his mother walked Sophia back to her room talking about what she needed to take for the trip to Camelot.

Sophia was a bit anxious how Kanani had done without her. She opened the door to her room, turned to say goodnight and thanked both of them for the lovely evening.

"I'll see you early in the morning, goodnight kind sir."

"Good night Lady Yglais, thank you for your hospitality."

"Good night my Lady," Lamorak and his mother both said, then they turned to walk away.

Sophia closed the door and screamed!!!!

ABOUT THE AUTHOR

MICHELE WRITES UNDER the pen name JMM Adams. She lives in the North West with her beloved German Shepherds, parrot and horse. A new Casey Lane and Jackie Lee Mystery is in the works.

Be sure to catch all of the blogs and updates on new material on Facebook under Author JMM Adams, twitter and www.jmmadams.com

Michele appreciates her fans and friends for loving her characters as much as she does.

88653916R00189

Made in the USA
Columbia, SC
08 February 2018